Clifford Henry Beans Kitchen 1895-1967

STREAMERS WAVING

The Landmark Library

STREAMERS WAVING

C.H.B. Kitchin

"But who is this? What thing of sea or land –
Female of sex it seems –
That, so bedecked, ornate, and gay,
Comes this way sailing,
Like a stately ship . . .
With all her bravery on, and tackle trim,
Sails filled, and streamers waving."
MILTON: *Samson Agonistes*

"Vers une mer glaciale." ANDRE GIDE

CHATTO & WINDUS
LONDON

Published by
Chatto & Windus Ltd
London

*

Clarke, Irwin & Co. Ltd
Toronto

ISBN 0 7011 1975 6

First published in 1925
This edition first published in 1973

Printed in Great Britain by
Redwood Press Limited
Trowbridge, Wiltshire

To
My God-Fathers
W.H.B.
D.B.K.

I

Lydia Clame said :

" Then it came to me, all in a flash, that Geoffrey had gone to India with the Green-Travers girl. My harangue (as I explained to the crowds thronging the rostrum) was a funeral oration. ' Beneath that charming and whimsical personality of his,' I told them, ' he concealed the man he was.' If these words sounded odd to my audience, they sounded even odder to me. What did I mean ? The phrase was forced upon me."

" You could tell us at great length what you did not mean——" said Mr. Homfray.

Miss Clame began to do so, but he stopped her.

" Has Miss Gweller interpreted your dream ? "

" Not to my satisfaction. You see, by ' the man he was ' I didn't mean to indicate the conventional manly virtues, hope, fortitude, forbearance—whatever they may be."

" I fear you meant," said Mrs. Homfray, " that he wasn't quite a man."

" Oh, but he is. Besides, he might easily go to India."

To her three friends she was unintelligible, but by her last remark she had intended to refute the argument that a visit to India by Geoffrey was so unreal as to make nonsense of the rest of her dream.

Miss Gweller feared that the others had understood.

" Your garden, Mr. Homfray, is so lovely, that it hardly seems quite genuine."

" It is not genuine. It dates (except for the substratum, the soil, the area, the walls) from Tuesday, when Winckworth's installed it. Four van-loads of pots and a dozen stalwarts. You see we are abroad all the winter."

It was the third of April. For the moment warm sunshine drenched an orange umbrella planted in the middle of a brilliant lawn. Beneath the umbrella, in pale blue basket chairs, sat Mr. and Mrs. Homfray, Miss Gweller and Miss Clame. Mrs. Homfray poured out tea. A red lacquer cake-stand offered four kinds of sandwiches, currant bread and butter and a walnut cake iced violet. At each corner of the lawn was a quincunx of tropical palms. Between the quincunces and round each of them ran a ribbon of closely packed hyacinths, red and blue. There

8

was a raised bank at one end of the lawn, where tulips and narcissi, preternaturally tall, stood massed as if for a manœuvre. Even the violet was immodest. Beyond the bank, the river Thames flowed placidly towards Maidenhead. On the far side of the river the English trees (not supplied by Winckworth's) were wondering whether to risk their foliage.

The house to which the unreal garden was appended was called Elfindale. Its owners were Mr. and Mrs. Homfray. Mr. Homfray was Mrs. Homfray's second husband, she his first wife, and five years the senior. A niece of Mrs. Homfray named Miss Cooper had been at school with Miss Clame. Mrs. Homfray was a devoted aunt, and Miss Clame, a blushing little thing with two or three pig-tails, had often shared Miss Cooper's invitations. Then they matured and parted. The radiant Miss Cooper became Mrs. Lucas and died a year afterwards in attempting to perpetuate her new name. Miss Clame was out of touch and did not grieve excessively. But she was not quite forgotten, and three chance meetings with Mrs. Homfray (one in Stewart's, one in Harrod's and one at the Ideal Homes Exhibition at Olympia) culminated in a long week-end at Elfindale. As for Miss Gweller, one would not be surprised at seeing her anywhere. She had

9

long known Miss Clame, Mrs. Homfray and many more important people.

Miss Clame was accustomed to telling the story of her life. With palmistry, character improvisations at the piano and artificial respiration, it was one of her parlour accomplishments. She had an opening after tea, when Mr. Homfray asked if she lived alone in London.

Miss Gweller (who had all knowledge) replied first.

" Lydia lives with two spinsters, Mavina Trelawny, who nearly climbed Mont Blanc, and Godiva Smith, who colours pottery. You might call it Bloomsbury. 52 Beam Square—' m ' for Mussolini, not the vegetable."

" Indeed. There is quite a Bloomsbury set, is there not ? "

" There is," said Miss Clame, " but we're not in it. We're just the tiniest bit west, both spiritually and geographically. You remember my Aunt Dawes," she went on quickly, as if fearful of interruptions. " I was living with Aunt Dawes when you first knew me. I left her three years after I came into my five hundred a year. It's really five forty, thanks to Hipswell & Holtby, who pay ten per cent and bonus of two and a half. I'm always having tiffs with my trustees, who want to put the money into one of those dim government things which dwindle slowly. With my five forty I thought I could live quite comfortably, especially if I made a little extra by my various accomplishments. I can teach so many things. First I tried the piano, then dancing, then art. But my pupils were such jammy half-crowners. Why should I bother, after all ? So I do nothing, except a little in the house. Since Deevie (Godiva, you know) wanted a studio, Anna sleeps out. There are advantages in that, though."

" And your evenings, child ? Do you read—embroider ? "

" Oh, I'm not often in. I get a good many 'after dinners'. I dance, play all card games, even act. And we have our own parties. Some of them might almost be put into inverted commas. Not that I care for looseness."

" You have a large acquaintance ? "

" I grade them in three groups—eleven bosom friends, sixty pleasant acquaintances and over two hundred and fifty 'people I know'. Mostly feminine, though. I'm not in society. The artistic sets take no cognisance of me. And smartness appals me. Still, we have our eccentricities. The fringe of the mantle of Princess Vayadère brushes our way now and then—famous in three continents for her incontinence, as Reggie Muswell puts it. You may well shiver. And I was at the eldest Green-Travers' wedding."

She paused and stroked a black cat that approached her with elaborate gestures.

" Do they see one another much ? " asked Miss Gweller.

" So Isabel Peverett tells me."

" These names—and the absence of them— are lost on us, you know," said Mrs. Homfray.

" Puss, puss, bring me luck. It's nothing, Mrs. Homfray. You see, I'm thirty. I have my skeletons."

" There is a Sir Archbold Peverett who has kindly sent us tickets for the launching of the giant submarine on Whit Tuesday."

" I shall be there," said Miss Gweller.

" And the day after, we have to see the start of Billy Demble's flight to the South Pole."

" I couldn't manage both," said Miss Gweller.

" I adore the summer and its refreshment tents. One day in autumn I shall die casually. It will be a great and sudden blow for my friends."

" Bosom friends," Mrs. Homfray corrected her.

" By Christmas Day, though, I shall be quite outlived."

" Do you hanker for immortality ? "

" Not really. I like the open air, and parks and bands playing in the distance."

" We are wondering where to go after the season," said Mr. Homfray. " We have tried every country in Europe except Denmark."

" I have been to Copenhagen nine times," put in Miss Gweller. " Once less than to *Madame Butterfly*. As for Christiania, it is the dullest capital in Europe—Helsingfors always excepted. Now if only Leningrad were available ! "

" Yes, the North draws us this year."

Miss Clame sighed.

" August is always insoluble, till it is over."

" But making plans, don't you think, is half the joy ? "

" I always seem," said Miss Clame, " to have just been doing something, or to be just going to do something. Never actually to be doing anything."

" That is a sad and important truth about life. We drift from deed to deed."

The sun vanished behind clouds, and a wind wailed in the palm-trees. The village clock struck.

" Two minutes slow," said Miss Gweller, looking at her watch.

" You, or it ? "

" I have had this watch twenty-three years. It has never yet failed me."

A shower of sleet fell resoundingly upon the umbrella, out of which the four tea-drinkers dashed to the french window of the dining-room.

" Puss, puss," wistfully called Miss Clame. But despite the hail, the attraction of the sand-wiches was too strong. Disconsolate, she followed her host and hostess and Miss Gweller indoors. In August where would she be, and what would she be doing ?

II

THE little cretonne curtain, hardly yet even an undistinguished pink, flapped fitfully against Miss Clame's window, hygienically ajar. A sullen dawn, or rather more—for it was a good while after sunrise—filtered into the angles of the room.

Miss Clame turned in bed. "Risest thou thus?" she thought. It was just the morning on which Anna would fail. An evil morning, fine at the outset, but full of menace. (The horror of tiptoe-ing in bedroom slippers, elegant but thin, over the cold bathroom linoleum!) The matches would have disappeared, unlike those half-dozen cups and saucers, smirched with the cocoa of the night before. One would be on the mantelpiece, another lopsidedly on the divan, a third on the piano. Methodically she posed the whole set. They say that if the landlord provides constant hot water it saves you twenty-five pounds a year. It would have been worth it to take the flat in Smith Street. (The universe contains no problems, but many details.) Of course, if one were used to it, one could get up without a cup of weak tea and two slices of brown bread and butter.

The curtain flapped with fresh vigour. " Come in." Miss Clame turned over in bed, opened her eyes and looked at the window and its unfamiliar curtain with sleepy incredulity, as if expecting it, like a discord, to resolve itself. Then she blinked with satisfaction and turned over once more. The beds at Elfindale were good. Did Mrs. Homfray go to Heal's or the new place in Oxford Street? One simply rested without being smothered. How marvellous it would be if one could make all one's faculties become supreme merely by resting them. Why not stay in bed for six weeks? People did it, but they were ill. Otherwise, it would be called pathological. Reggie had said that Jenny was pathological. Well, after all, no one is made of ice.

What was it she had said the other day? " Beneath that charming and whimsical personality of his, he concealed the man he was." The words might almost have been printed in italics in a little mauve pamphlet. " In Memoriam G. R. Oration by Lydia Clame." It was an ominous and unaccountable fancy. It might be possible to tell him about it, with a very light touch. On no account be ostentatious—a postage stamp with no gum on the back. Well, there was gum on her back, if he liked to. . . . Crude, crude. No wonder people dubbed her a dear pert little thing. A chrysalis stage, which straightway she would outgrow. From that day forward there should be no nonsense. A true woman, dignified and serene, nourishing a secret sorrow. " Who ? Oh yes, I know that. I advised him. She's a pretty girl and has, of course, a position. We talked it over for a long time."

One, get Miss Beeler in for Wednesday. Two, order the new notepaper. Three, speak to Mavina about not using the butter-knife. Four, refuse the Peveretts. At least, answer Mrs. Peverett. What was the fifth ? The osprey ? No. The storyette for *Astarte* ? No. Something to do with bees. The flapping curtain reminded her. (When bees swarm, one beats things. Was there a special apparatus ? Swarm-settlers, tin, one and three : galvanised iron, two and eleven. Surely it was in Gamage's catalogue.) " Dear Mr. Durrant—I regret to have to write again—it is with much regret that I write a second time—to inform you that the cowl on the chimney above my bedroom still makes its incessant and offensive noise. It might, in fact, be a swarm-settler. I trust you will at

once take all steps necessary to abate this nuisance."
It was a real legal phrase according to Reggie.
What a time he had dallied with his profession.
Twenty-nine, and still no brief. What a time
we all waste by waiting. Twenty-nine. Thirty.
Thirty-one comes less abruptly. "She's in the
thirties." "Really? As much as that?" Or
better, "Rot, what cats you women are. If she's
a day over twenty-five, I'll eat my hat." Not
quite a Siegfried's phrase.

> "Mir strahlt zur Stunde Siegfrieds Stern :
> Er ist mir ewig, ist mir immer
> Erb' und Eigen, Ein' und All . . ."

There was a knock, and the door opened.

"Mrs. Homfray suggests that you might like
your breakfast brought up, Miss."

"Dear, dear. Is it so late?"

"No, Miss, by no means. Barely eight,
Miss."

"Is it any consequence?"

(Miss Clame meant inconvenience. Powerful
as was the soliloquy of her thoughts, she was not
capable yet of fluency with the world outside
her.)

"It's usual here, Miss, if I may say so."

"That will be splendid."

"And should you like a cup of tea now, Miss?
And a little bread and butter?"

" Indeed, yes."

" And at what hour shall I prepare your bath, Miss ? "

" Oh, let me see. When would it——? "

" The water's boiling now, Miss."

" Very well. In a quarter of an hour. Say ten minutes after you bring my tea."

" Thank you, Miss."

" Miss Gweller, is she——? "

" Miss Gweller's up and abroad, Miss."

" Abroad ? "

" She went out by the side-door into the garden, and looked at the boats. Then she came in, passed through the front hall and out she went into the road—and it seemed more like snowing than anything."

" I trust she takes no cold."

" Amen, Miss. And now I'll be getting your tea."

" Thank you so much. Thank you."

" At your service, Miss."

Miss Clame once more became inert. " Dear Mr. Durrant," she began. Then the word " swarm-settler " obtruded itself again, and at the thought of it she laughed with little internal ripples, as she had not laughed since she had discovered in church (by looking at a red morocco prayer-book) that Miss Gweller's brother's name was Gwyllyth. She had laughed all through the sermon. A very queer sermon it was, too. Terribly nautical. " Then they rounded Cyprus, and by dint of undergirding the vessel, anchored off Antioch. . . . Research has shown that at Antioch there were two harbours, one of which was reserved for what (without disrespect) we may term the Roman Royal Mail Packets. . . ." (The harbour at Antioch, all done up in red plush and labelled RESERVED.) The only time when Reggie Muswell was ever caned at school, was for laughing in Chapel. He disturbed the worship of the masters' wives. " A sacrilegious guffaw," the Headmaster had said.

Another knock at the door. Miss Clame sat up.

" Your tea, Miss. And shall I draw the curtains, Miss ? "

" Thank you. If you would be so good."

" There's a bit more promise in the day, Miss, now."

" Yes, indeed."

" In ten minutes, Miss, I'll have your bath prepared."

" Thank you. I shall be quite ready."

What a change these country servants were.

Four shillings might do. It was not as if Elfindale were a smart house—like Bridalstone or Moulton Bassett Manor, for instance. Still, the Homfrays had money to spend, and spent it. A florin and half-a-crown, perhaps. A florin for the chauffeur, and the rail-fare eight and nine. For four days, it was an economy. Delicious tea. The habit of week-ending was altogether charming. It had a distinction. "Yes, any day. Though, of course, I'm usually out of town from Friday to Monday. Rather a bore I find it. I do so envy you people who can stroll down a deserted Throgmorton Street."

Her tea finished, Miss Clame rose, donned a dressing-gown of pale green crepe with a beaded sash, and went to the window. How radiant a morning! Yet the wind was chilly and the middle palm-tree in the farthest quincunx had fallen on to its side, and clawed the air with feverish green fingers. The Remingtons were motoring over to lunch from Moulton Bassett. Lady Cecilia, Mr., Gwennie and Blanche, that was to say. Then they were all to go to Bridalstone for tea and perhaps tennis. There, Geoffrey might look in. What could he be doing, floating about so elusively in that neighbourhood? Did all London rush to the Thames valley in April? Surely Surrey was more *à la mode*. But then these people weren't really in the creamy set. Tea and perhaps tennis. That permitted some latitude in costume.

"Your bath, Miss."

(Nail-brush, loofah and sponge.)

"Shall I find a towel?"

"Yes, Miss. And what do you fancy for your breakfast, Miss?"

(Soap.)

"An apple, a lightly boiled egg, bread and butter, toast and marmalade, tea and plenty of hot water."

"The second door on the left, Miss."

Why, that was Mr. Homfray lathered up to the eyes, with the dressing-room door wide open.

Over the bath stood Queen Victoria framed in black and gold.

III

He had come, with a sudden whirring of gears in the drive, just as they were finishing tea on the terrace at Bridalstone. All eyes had swept over the rhododendrons. There was a scamper towards the hall.

"It's only Geoffrey," said Blanche. "He fusses round like a revolving door. What a set people make at him."

"We have," Lady Cecilia Remington said to Miss Gweller, "a more than usually elusive son."

Sir Claude Browne did not like the younger generation.

"The curse of modern locomotion, Cecilia. The motor-car replaces the wife and severs the parental tie."

At the side of the house there was a babel of voices.

"Oh, that's all right, I'll leave Lumbago in the drive."

"Still the same old bus?"

"Thank God you've changed."

"Cold? Why, it's simply boiling."

" Come on at once. Nobody else cares two-pence."

A white group (as in *Les Sylphides*) fluttered from the wings on to the tennis lawn. Then by an adroit turn in the chorography, Geoffrey was left alone in the middle of the net. He wore a white alpaca coat (with a mauve device on the breast pocket), white trousers, socks and shoes. As he bent down to measure the height of the net, the pipe in his mouth gave a pucker to his short fair moustache. In the sunlight, his hair gleamed.

Miss Clame crossed her hands in her lap.

" Another cup, Miss Clame ? Aren't they absurd ? You're so wise none of you to have come changed. My daughters are maniacs."

" I suppose they go in for tournaments, Lady Browne ? "

(How flat a remark ! As if all the world didn't go in for tournaments. Why not have said " For me, tennis is but a perversion of ping-pong " ? But that was not in the Bridal-stone manner. Harmonise. Away with jarring notes.)

" In the autumn we have two tournaments, one for our friends and one for our tenants. Last year Janet won both. I was quite ashamed."

" Now can I book you for July, Miss Gweller ?

Positively, you must visit us. It's Geoffrey's birthday on the eighth. I dare hardly think what we shall be up to."

" As long as it doesn't clash with Wimbledon, Henley or the golf, Lady Cecilia, I should love to come. As a matter of fact, my brother will be with me . . ."

" Would he come too ? We should be more than charmed."

" If it's all right about his hair—he has a treatment always during those two weeks . . ."

" What, during Wimbledon ? "

" He sets small store, I fear, by outdoor sports. His heart is in his stamp-album."

Pearls before swine. An eternity descended on the bevy round the tea-table. " It's not as if we were still eating," thought Miss Clame. " I wait, I wait as always for the next move. Check to the queen. A pawn can protect a knight. I am too quick for these players. They dawdle. Sometimes, alas, they win ! "

" May I admire those daffodils, Lady Browne ? "

" Yes, indeed. They make a pretty show. But from what I hear of Elfindale, we must deprecate comparisons."

" One of the big palms," whispered Miss Clame, " was blown down in the night."

" H'm. No doubt it will soon be replaced."

The strategic position of the daffodil bank made Miss Clame's admiration of it unconscionably long. At length, when she had twice noted every blighted bloom, every warped leaf, there was a pause in the tennis which reorganised. Nearer and nearer came Geoffrey to the bank, yet with a circular movement like a ball attached by a string of rubber to a waving stick and flung outwards with a jerk. At any moment there might be a rebound.

" Hello, Miss Clame ! Fancy finding you here ! "

(Every impression must be registered, every word printed indelibly within. Here at last was fresh food for sleepless nights, fresh substance out of which to weave shadows, fresh reality on which to frame an ecstasy. Speech deserted her.)

" Are you staying with the Brownes ? " he went on.

" No, with the Homfrays at Elfindale. Do you know them ? "

" I think I do. Why don't you come over and see us ? "

" I should love to."

" I've got to go to Surrey to-morrow, though, and Lumbago, my old bus, can't do more than fifteen m.p.h."

" The Green-Travers ? "

" Yes.   Betty's twenty-firster.   I suppose you'll be in town most of the season ? "

" All of it, during the week."

" Are you going to the Peveretts on the twenty-fourth ?   Mrs. Peverett's my godmother, and I've been so beastly rude to her lately that I've simply got to go.   Do turn up.   I want to see some one I know."

" Yes, I'll be there.   Do you remember Jenny Sale ? "

" The young person in jade ? "

(It was not his own phrase.)

Three importunate voices welled up from the background.

" Geoffrey !   Geoff !   It'll be dark if we don't get on with it."

" Sorry," he shouted backwards, shook hands, waved gaily and sped to the net.

Miss Clame observed a little juniper tree with hostility.   What an idiotic remark.   " It'll be dark if we don't get on with it."   Illogical in the extreme.   As if " getting on with it " made any difference to the sunset, regulated months in advance by one's diary.   Damn Adela, Janet and Jennifer.   " The Duke of Barnsborough calls them the three graces," Lady Browne used to say.   Three screaming hussies.   Six angular legs, sixty thousand freckles between them. The bridges of their noses seemed almost dirty. Their stupidity passed belief. Cheltenham would have none of them. To Girton could they not aspire. " As daffodils to a dahlia, so they are to me," she thought. But some people admire daffodils.

Miss Gweller approached and took Miss Clame's arm.

" We're to be going," she said.

" At once ? "

" I've never been able to place the Brownes, have you ? "

" I've never tried."

" I don't think they'll go far. Lady Cecilia is a charming woman. Come on, you nymph. Are you attached to the soil ? "

"I loathe it. Over my new shoes, too. Are they waiting ? "

" Hours and hours."

" Lydia ! " said Mrs. Homfray from the terrace.

" The worst of gardens is," said Miss Clame, " that they're always full of people shouting for one another."

They marched back to the terrace and round to the front door.

" Now," said Mr. Homfray when they had settled in the car, " what do you say to a little run round by Humblebird Church ? It has a wonderful decagonal porch, and just one perfect bit of stained glass. We can do it in time to miss vespers (if there is such a service to-day). I should have taken you there this morning, but the glass is absolutely invisible except at this time in the afternoon when the sun is in an appropriate position."

" I saw Humblebird Church this morning," said Miss Gweller.

" This morning ? "

" I rose at seven."

" Well, indeed ! But not the glass ? "

" The glass is being repaired."

" Architecture bores me," said Mrs. Homfray. " It is an art without a soul."

" Well then, straight home, Tiffin."

Even despite the most careful manœuvring, the mud-guard of the Homfrays' Daimler grazed Lumbago, sprawling like a decrepit star-fish in the drive.

" He's a devil-may-care harum-scarum," said Mr. Homfray.

Saturday, Sunday, Monday. Then Tuesday and Beam Square. It was a long way off.

IV

At last Oxo gave place to Bovril, Bovril to Pears' Soap. Buffet faded and gentlemen waned. Alone, the telegraph wires kept pace, lowering themselves as if in a caress, until with a flash of vertical blackness they were recalled to the dignity of their first altitude. The compartment, which Miss Clame had to herself, smelt of ectoplasm.

"Doctor," she would say, "I cannot sleep. For three nights I have been sleepless. I am overstrung."

"Can you particularise your symptoms? Shall I examine you?"

"My symptoms, doctor, are mental. They are of the brain. Not, I mean, that my faculties are impaired. I am still lucid. I can multiply, divide, apportion the rent, read Scriabin at sight, translate from the Russian, tell a genuine Gorgione a furlong off. But I am listless, drowsy, spiritually numb. My nerves are agog. The openings and shuttings of doors bewilder me. The sight of a lady-bird makes me faint. The scent of a rosebud puts me to shame. I am weary of life."

" A little saline of a morning, my dear lady . . ."

" No, doctor. I am open to no facile cure. Physically, I am a marvel. My plight is graver. My repartees fail me. My gestures no longer express me. My thoughts are turbulent and disordered, cohesive, clotted, no longer a calm melodious flow of intelligence. My charm dwindles. My wits are ageing, my deportment that of a child."

" All this society life you ladies will lead tells on you in the end. Rest and solitude will work wonders. Cancel all engagements until August."

" That is the one month, doctor, when I have no engagement. My pique would madden me. In my sleep I should haunt the Berkeley, during massage envisage Hurlingham."

" Have you a worry, a millstone on the mind ? "

" My independence, doctor, is complete. Unfitted by training and temperament for life's more onerous duties, I am left free for the cult of self-enjoyment. I have a great capacity for pleasure. Provided with (thanks to Hipswell & Holtby) over five hundred a year, no relatives to whom I must account, no occupation, no scruples, a comfortable home, charming companions, I should soar through existence, a veritable albatross of de-light. Yet what am I ? A caged linnet, an ass in the shafts, a glow-worm climbing up an arc-lamp."

" Dear lady, are you in love ? "

It was a time for tears.

All the way from Slough past the Dolphin signal-box and the Home Counties Bacon Factory to Langley (Bucks) she wept, the sly tears rolling out like little sins in a confessional. Miss Clame in love ! What would each one of them say ?

" Such a frivolous little thing."

" Try bicycling."

" Come with me my next slumming-day."

" Again ? " (That would be Ruth Gweller.)

" Give boldly. Be proud and open in your passion." (Deevie.)

" Is she not past the age ? "

At Langley (Bucks) she became more cerebral. After all, determination knows no barriers. (Office-boy to impressario, ice-man to rail-road king.) The will was there already, but there remained strategies to be considered, tactics planned, technique mastered. Assuredly, she must read Stendhal and *La Vie Parisienne*. Abler than any of her acquaintances, why should she fail ?

These overweening Green-Travers must be humbled, Betty above all. With Princess Vayadère, something might be done. A word in that quarter would not stay there for long. The Princess was a star, but have not stars their perigees? Up and play the comet, the bold intruder. "Princess, my visit may surprise you. . . . Unfortunately it is as obligatory for me as it will be diverting to you. . . . One of your friends, Princess, is worse than faithless. . . . I mention no names, but in setting her cap . . ." Then would follow the story, a series of bold brush-strokes till the canvas reeked. Or else a Scribe-Legouvé "Bataille des Dames." "My intelligence and wit, my fragile charm against her hoydenish healthiness. In cow-milking, maybe, I am no match for her : at lacrosse, my lustre is dimmed. But question me on Schopenhauer, income-tax, counter-point or the price of lampreys. Confront me with an electorate. No fist will daunt me, no argument leave me tongue-tied." And all this must be divined rather than said. As an aroma it must irradiate (scent and light mingled in a higher unity) her person, her apartment, her path through the world. A strenuous course of before-breakfast exercises seemed necessary.

Over the devoured line, the houses cast long shadows. Every second, Beam Square with its two or three backgrounds (foggy December mornings, otiose and unending Sunday afternoons, hot summer evenings of intolerable tension) loomed more largely. In the living-room ("our parlour," they called it), like love-birds playing at nests, would be Deevie full length on the mauve divan or even, cushioned with pale blue and *tête de nègre*, on the buff floor. She would be looking upwards, as if a naughty picture were set in the ceiling. Mavina might well be on the window-sill, by her adventurous pose giving it the look of a crag on the Matterhorn. Her eyes, turned through the window, would almost penetrate the soil of the square garden-plot, as if inflamed with longing to uproot the weeds that had not yet pierced the surface. Her conversation (at least, in what it left unspoken) was a clumsy version of the *Georgics*. When it rained, her lips seemed framed to utter "Rake and hoe," no less than they enjoined sweepings of dead leaves, prunings and transplantings, when autumn winds were blowing. Frost on the ground was for her a symbol of buttressed celery, June mellowness of the adhesive pea. What with "lambings" and "calvings" and her knowledge of poultry-yards she would bring a blush to Chelsea Hospital.

Miss Clame regarded both of them as tolerably

suitable for her. She was outshone by neither. In Deevie there was a streak—more than a streak, said some—of vulgarity, which alternately amused and had to be discouraged. Miss Clame thanked Heaven that she was free from that. When with Lady Cecilia and other such, it would have been perpetually to be repressed. It was something to be the daughter of an army man and an army woman—for the late Mrs. Clame was the sixth daughter of a brigadier-general—even if they only left fourteen thousand between them. (Jane Austen would tell her readers this with perfect frankness. See the beginning of *Mansfield Park*. Nothing is so bourgeois as to be afraid to speak of money.)

Miss Clame was not ashamed of her small income, though it thwarted her about eight times a day. If she were wealthier she would probably not know Deevie or Mavina. It was no reflection upon them. But the Queen of Sheba cannot pose as a love-bird, or sprawl on a badly made mauve divan. (Miss Clame had always been against that divan, even if its absence meant the loss of atmosphere.) The Queen of Sheba would have real lion-skins and tiger-skins and ostrich plumes, and orgies suitable to her trappings. Poor Deevie never had orgies. It was hard for her even to raise an intrigue. Mavina did not want either. She was a captive. When she met a young man she would ask him about a new variety of phlox or the rhododendron that grows only on the Himalayas and in somebody's garden near Torquay. Well, the Jack and Mrs. Sprat principle was a very good one. It was a pity that Deevie could not be made more sexless. Perhaps by giving her special food the result might be achieved. (It was Miss Clame's turn to do the catering again.) Fortunately Deevie's ideal was a common young man with a loose mouth, cheekily familiar and physically forward. To her Geoffrey would mean less than Plotinus.

"On the whole," Miss Clame decided, as Paddington station swallowed up the train, "Deevie had better know nothing. I may say a little to Mavina, if the mood takes me. But now that I have discovered that I really am in love, I feel a healthy impulse to reticence. I was a little free with my dream at Elfindale, I think. But the Homfrays are of no account, and Ruth is one of those people who can only find a needle when it is in a haystack. Having persuaded herself that she is ' subtle '—for the implications of that word see Gide's *Les Caves du Vatican*—she has become a regular booby over the obvious. Several problems confront me. I must not fall between two stools. But I can hear Lady Browne saying to Lady Cecilia, ' Who is she ? ' and the reply, ' Oh, nobody at all.' What would Deevie say if I demanded to have my father's portrait over the mantelpiece ? She might produce her chocolate-boxy aunt. (Portrait of a woman of the lower middle class, *c.* 1880.) No, as I am living with them, I must be neat rather than gaudy. There is nothing I hate so much as snobbery. Perhaps because I have reason to fear it. . . ."

She settled into a taxi, amazed at her bold self-analysis. That was the style—a great advance upon " Doctor, I am overstrung." " First realise what you are," she told herself, " then what you wish to be. That is half the battle." . . . " Miss Clame returned to London on Tuesday afternoon, having spent a long week-end near Maidenhead. . . . A marriage has been arranged and will shortly take place. . . . Towards those in all ranks of society she has the same charming manner. . . . Your successes, Lydia, come without effort. . . . My dear Duchess, you flatter me. . . ."

Then came Beam Square, and another sleepless night.

V

THE park orator in the pea-soup sports coat had
been both to Oxford and Cambridge. He had
indeed been to several other universities, but
these were the only two against which he had a
grievance. Declamatory rather than popular, he
not infrequently had no audience at all. At half-
past three on the 24th of April, he had an audience
of one; for Miss Clame, holding her green little
umbrella at a military angle to her shoulder, was
listening to him as much as she was pretending
either to be elsewhere, or to be inanimate or
rooted to the spot, sapling or twopenny chair.

World-revolution, she thought, when prefixed
with the word " the " becomes doubly offensive.
It is at once, by the definite article, raised to the
category of inevitables—*the* deluge, *the* eclipse,
the Celtic revival. This was all wrong. One
should speak of *a* revolution, as one would
mention *a* flower-show, *a* broken vase, *an* erup-
tion of Vesuvius. These people had such scien-
tific conceit in their dogmatism—like Heraclitus
(was it ?) who said boldly, " The world is made

of water," without even noticing the avoided puddle. One knew exactly how their text-books would run. " History for beginners." " Eventually the red-hot nebula, which we call the earth, solidified and cooled. Man, first cousin of monkeys, developed from the amoeba. Having by reason of his whatnot (Latin words) dominated all other animals, he devoted himself to the elaboration of a system of capitalism and oppression, until repenting of his folly he made amends for his errors in the world-revolution, after which vanity, luxury and personal interest have been happily unknown, etc."

" And where do I come in, pray ? " thought Miss Clame, having heard that light unproductive women would burst as bubbles in the revolutionary sea and be heard of no more. " Are my emotions of no account ? Have the subtleties of my thoughts and desires no kinship with eternal beauty ? "

" Beauty," said the lecturer, " is a warped manifestation of the life-force. Woe to the parasite class, diseased in its imaginations and criminal in its pursuit of them."

" And yet," thought Miss Clame, " there must be at least a thousand professors in the world who give their lives to parasitology. Some even say that parasitism is a symbol of supreme intelligence. Since I exist, I have my place in the history of the world. Have I no page in your book, no saving paragraph? A thousand years hence, a million students will explore me. 'Let us now study the habits,' they will say, 'of Miss Clame. Let us investigate her rising, her breakfast, her morning task, her actions and reactions.' Indeed, the most imaginative will reconstruct this little walk of mine across the park, my eager yet desultory gait, my powder, my lip-stick, my knowledge of the future, my prediction of their curiosities, the curved contempt of my smile, this gesture which they will strive in vain to demonstrate."

"A cypher, a zero, a nullity," said the orator, "an effect, but a cause of nothing."

"Hoity-toity," she replied, by accident aloud, "I am the cause of the world-revolution. Admire me."

The orator paused, open-mouthed. (A wren could have popped in.) In the trees, the amorous birds twittered with a great garrulity. Peace descended upon Miss Clame. She closed her eyes, as if about to swoon, and wondered why.

"Three hundred and eighty-two thousand babies have, on an average, one bottle between fifty-three, while nine hundred and ninety-seven men have but one pair of braces amongst them."

Miss Clame blushed. "He heard me," she thought, "he must have heard me. He is ignoring me. He floods me with statistics. How odd I am, to wrangle in a public place, to be so affected by it all,—I who have two dressing-cases, forty-three handkerchiefs and all Voltaire in a very special binding."

Her back was eloquent, as she strode southward. No doubt there was a taxi-stand in Park Lane, but there was also one at Hyde Park Corner. (Ten to one they all faced the wrong way. How often had the turn meant an extra threepence.) The bus-top was better for the homeward journey. No, it was not snobbishness. ("I adore the bedroom-window level.") But a smut in the corner of the eye is no joke, while the expelling tear would surely leave a redness. And the footman, if one appears before him titivating, announces one in the wrong voice—all the accent on the "Miss," and invariably after *Lady* Hayway and before *Dame* Hildegard Brookfield. "*Ss Clame*," it should be said, or even "*Sclame*." "We're so glad you could come." "Why, Lydia, is it you?" "It's good to see you again." "Come here, you sweet oasis."

The phrases rippled with her steps. She barely knew Mrs. Peverett. "Do you ever see your cousin Hamilton? Where is he now?"

41

" Of that I have not the least idea." " I expect you know everybody here. That is the Princess Vayadère." " Indeed ? I thought that, for the moment, since her name appeared in so many papers——" " And General Osgood is dying to meet you—a great friend of your father's. (Beware, my dear, these interesting bachelors.) " Then Mrs. Peverett would ogle. It was all very shallow. But of the depths one could neither speak nor think. Hail Siegfried !

Forest murmurs resounded westwards in the Park, while on the left a confusion of motor-horns might have been bagpipes at a gathering of the clans. Miss Clame recollected Inverness and its pale so Scottish river flowing beneath a tepid northern sun. How the kilt had flapped on the dancer's lifted knee ! Bannocks and shortbread, oatcake, scons or scoans (pronounced, whichever way was correct, in an un-English fashion). But the men had talked too much of fishing, and she had been immature. There was a chill north of the Tweed, for all the delightful honesty and cleanliness of that admirable people. Still, it would be attractive to have Inverness at hand, just where Hertford Street drifted into a dreary nothingness, for example. Replace the Marble Arch by the Arc de Triomphe, the Achilles statue by the Bismarck Denkmal at Hamburg, or

the portentous effigy that commands the railway
running opposite Coblentz, Piccadilly by the
Promenade des Anglais or Strandvägen, the
Serpentine by the Grand Canal. It would indeed be an enchantment to step thus from atmosphere to atmosphere, pole to pole. No other
fantasy was more likely to destroy those longings
wasteful and wistful, which perpetually embraced
the absent. How many lives might one not
unite by those transitions—how many adventures ? And how many deaths could one not
afford to die ?

She had reached Hyde Park Corner, and pon-
dered a line of taxis fronting eastwards. With
her umbrella she waved to the first one, although
for comfort and cleanliness of paint she judged
that the third could not be rivalled. Its driver,
too, was more reassuring. Youths with those
cloth-capped ears are not disposed to open doors
to you. But it was the first taxi which came to
her, inexorably ticking, as it manœuvred in a
clumsy semicircle to the pavement.

VI

Miss Clame was early, and the footman gave full weight to both the monosyllables of her description. Of the small assembly, beyond Mrs. Peverett (no relation to, but in her own estimation far more important than, the Sir Archbold Peverett who gave tickets to the Homfrays), a few of her daughters and a big man with a drooping grey moustache (whom she suspected rather than knew), she knew nobody.

" You do know General Osgood, don't you ? " said the hostess. " He has wanted to meet you so much. I told him that I expected you here this afternoon, though I have no confidence in your ill-mannered generation."

" Mrs. Peverett," said Miss Clame with the gallantry of a young man, " how could I fail you ? Yes, I am sure I have met the General before."

He bowed and smiled like a contented cat, suggested tea, and when she postponed it, conveyed her to an alcove. From her position she could see the door.

" I knew your father," he said, glancing all

44

over her as if to prove her paternity. " You see, I am very, very old."

" My father was a young man when he died."

" We called him ' Binnie.' Did you know ? "

Anecdotes of the old days followed. At the door, radiantly strange, stood Princess Vayadère. Miss Clame divined her undertone, " Now whom have you got for me this afternoon ? " Mrs. Peverett was evidently mentioning several names.

" What does he do ? " the Princess asked imperiously.

" Well, the last we heard was the diplomatic, but I think it has fallen through."

Miss Clame resumed her own conversation.

" It was you, wasn't it, who sent father those four Bristol glass candlesticks ? One of them has already come to me. On the death of my aunt I get two more. The fourth was broken by our dove, years ago."

" Oh, I am sorry. I feel you should have them all. Let me make up the set for you."

Yes, she noted mechanically, that was Geoffrey in light snuff. His pockets bulged with graceful uncouthness. No doubt his pipe was there. He would smoke his pipe in and out of season. He did exactly as he liked, whimsical rather than overbearing.

" Oh, my dear General, I'm afraid I've lost the thread."

" I was asking about Mr. Homfray's pictures. I hear he has disposed of his Landseers."

" There is still one on the landing at Elfindale, I think."

" Should you not like some tea ? "

Now was the moment for Ruth Gweller to detain the Princess. The alcove was anything but a vantage point, and until after tea there was clearly no deliverance. How often, she thought, had she not been compelled to rest immobilised watching others move according to the dictates of their own wills or some communal exigency. It had been thus at Bridalstone, and at countless other parties.

" These, the flag tells me, are egg and cress, these shrimp and crab, these *foie gras.*"

" No caviare ? "

" I will see, but I don't think so."

Now was the moment for Geoffrey to pass Daisy Peverett on to Randolph Groves—how had he risen to the Peveretts ?—waiting for her on one toe. He did so, and sauntered towards the alcove with an air of careful blindness that was favourable. But the big hawk was swift to pounce. Down swept the Princess, both hands outspread as if in blind man's buff.

46

" Mr. Remington, do let me introduce myself. Your mother and mine were great friends. My name is Helen Vayadère."

She paused, her back to Miss Clame, who surmised her heaving bosom, widened eyes, flashing nostrils and triangular red smile. Geoffrey murmured and fumbled, and the Princess went on :

" It is so intriguing, don't you think, to meet some one of whom one has heard a great deal and then to form one's own impressions and to discover for oneself, not a complete difference, but a difference which means just everything to one—the Tintoretto turned to Titian, as it were. Let us sit down and talk one another over."

Where was the General ? Would he never come back for his dismissal ? Mrs. Peverett had once more assailed him. Miss Clame's faculties were paralysed, as they always were, by the nearness of the brilliant woman. On to the polished floor ebbed her vitality. Though she were instantly to have been electrocuted, she could not have moved. When Reggie Muswell came up with a much soiled collar, she barely flickered recognition to him. But he had his own emotions.

" I've just come," he said, " fresh from my first brief. I have to draft an agreement for the tenancy of a drain. In course of time I shall get two guineas. How are you ? "

47

" I live," she said, using a formula which had made her unpopular with more than one American. " Tell me about your drain."

" It involves an easement both of way and water. The case is further complicated because the local authority has given notice to repair."

" Do you ever have divorce cases ? " asked Miss Clame, hoping that her words would carry.

" I feel," the Princess was saying, " whenever I meet some one for the first time, just as a bee must feel when a clever gardener brings a newly invented flower from the greenhouse and tries it in a bed. Some day, I am sure, I shall find some really rare and original honey. That's what makes it worth while, buzzing round these pistils and pollens—please don't construe me too botanically—and getting one's wings from time to time a little sticky with the wrong stuff. Don't you feel that too ? "

Neither Geoffrey nor Miss Clame sustained their halves of their respective dialogues with much character.

" As for Chopin," said Reggie Muswell, " I have got over all my old distaste. I can imagine nothing more miraculous than to be brought up exclusively on Haydn's, Mozart's and Beethoven's piano sonatas till one's sixteenth birthday, and then suddenly to be introduced to Chopin's

études. You know the one in G flat major
which goes der da da, der da da, der da da, der da
da, or the one in F major which goes da da dum,
da da dum, da da dum. I'm sorry I can't quite
indicate it. I'm sure all this modern music
dazzles us much less than they were dazzled the
first time they heard Chopin in the forties, or
whenever it was. I feel that when people grow
older and have had their fill of Brahms' thickness,
Mozart's thinness, Beethoven's clumsy pomposity,
when they're too tired to listen to Bach and too
used up for Wagner, they all will come back in
the end to Schumann and Chopin, played quietly
and brightly on the piano, and meaning everything just because they pretend to say so little."

" Mightn't one feel the same about Grieg or
Verdi ? " asked Miss Clame, as the names came
biddably into her head.

" Grieg ? A mountebank, like Dvořák and
Liszt. Verdi, a declamatory charlatan. They
have no conciseness, no neatness, no wit, none
of the drawing-room manner."

" I will now give you my card," said the
Princess. " You must come to my next Thursday—about five. Or we should get to know
one another better if we saw one another alone
first, shouldn't we ? Come to lunch to-morrow,
and we'll drive to Hampton Court or the Monu-

ment—any of those places which they only know of in the Provinces."

Geoffrey's reply was inaudible, but the Princess said warningly as she moved away, " Mind, you mustn't think that my heart is a tenement," and she stretched out a hand which Geoffrey lamentably failed to kiss.

Miss Clame rose, only to be caught again by General Osgood, whose apologies were amplified by a whisky and soda. They talked until Miss Clame's insteps ached with the desire to tread new soil. At last, with a desperate sally she freed herself, in time to catch Geoffrey edging to the door. His pipe was in his mouth.

" Hello," he said.

Miss Clame could say nothing.

" I've been wanting to talk to you," he said, " but you were always in some one's clutches. Who was that woman I got cornered with ? "

" She was a Miss Trumper. Then, for about eighteen months she was the Princess Vayadère."

" Is she divorced ? " he said, his eyes full of a calm blue. (It was a fine moment.)

" No, but indefinitely separated."

" Well, I shouldn't wonder."

" Mr. Remington, do you remember Jenny Sale ? "

" No, I don't think so."

" Three weeks ago you called her the young person in jade."

" Oh yes, of course."

" She's going to dance at a little At Home we're having—not an At Home, a reception simply, a small gathering. It's quite informal, and one comes dressed or not, just as one likes. I wish you could be there."

(" The 12th of May." " Oh, what a pity, I shall be in Surrey then." " I am so sorry; come another time." " I should love to. But I shan't be much in town this season.")

By a merciful accident (to secure which Miss Clame might well have told innumerable beads), the hideous colloquy was averted. Instead, Geoffrey pulled out his engagement book and looked through it in anything but a secretive fashion. Miss Clame's quick eye caught a London engagement on May the 13th and another on May 15th.

" It is to be on May the 14th," she said. " It is a—a Wednesday."

" That will be most charming. Let me see. No, I have nothing down. At what time ? "

" At ten o'clock. You know where I live ? 52 Beam Square."

" Bean ? "

" B-e-a-m — for Ramsay MacDonald. You

51

can't miss it. You go straight up Tottenham Court Road, and it's on the——"

" I know. I had a—a friend once at number —er—very near there. Well, good-bye ; on the fourteenth—if we don't meet before."

He disappeared gaily into the vestibule.

It was an exquisite sunset.

VII

It was an exquisite sunset—but the sun on the following morning hardly seemed to rise, so dull and colourless was the day. The greatest artistic principle may be, as Miss Clame often declared, condensation—compression, not curtailment of substance. (Oxo cube and Bovril bottle.) There are few epics (she would in her didactic way continue) which might not more profitably be expressed as Sonnet Sequences, few quatrains which were not happier as couplets. How much more compendious is not the dramatic form, with its brackets and italics, than that of the novel, with its " he saids " and " she saids," descriptions and meditations ? How much more admirable is a simultaneity of meanings than a succession of them—Paul Claudel than Sir Walter Scott, for instance ? As the world grows older, time grows shorter, and everything else (except life) too long. *L'Heure Espagnole* we can still stomach, though *The Ring* and *The Magic Flute* exhaust us. The headline supersedes the leading article, and a causerie by Mr. Walkley Marcel Proust.

Artistically speaking, the period between the 24th of April and the 14th of May was lamentable. What a chance, here, for life to have condensed itself, to have united the few and dim sensations of those irrelevant days into one attempted spasm, and then, turning over a new page, as it were, to have come straight to the business of that highly coloured little poem which Miss Clame was all eagerness to read! But the contrary occurred. The noisy cowl above Miss Clame's bedroom still clattered, in spite of Mr. Durrant's letters. Miss Beeler still had to be sent for to do the sewing. By Mavina, the use of the butter-knife was still ignored. Over the new note-paper controversy waxed fiercely. ("Who knows how long we shall all be here?" asked Deevie, just as three times a year, once in each heat-wave, she would say, "My love is pure!" and sit for an hour or two afterwards with folded hands and an exasperating smile.)

Routine—to some the desk at nine, to others the plough at six—weighed on Miss Clame in spite or by reason of all her freedom. But existence was her business, and she was never idle. Perhaps she had busy hands and an idle heart. Yet in her heart she had no freedom. It was too grievously in thrall.

To speed the uncondensed days was now a task. Many and various were the expedients which she devised. The whole period being by reason of its length intractable, she divided it into fixed and manageable portions, each ending with a landmark which to her deliberately short-sighted gaze seemed the end of the whole series. Some of the landmarks depended upon the natural order of things. " Before that Wednesday," she would advise herself, " we shall have gained ten minutes in the evening. Till the middle of the entrée, we shall not need to light the candles." Again, more hazardously and indefinitely, " By that Wednesday the laburnum tree in the garden of the square will have begun to bloom." And so she would continue, using the future perfect tense vigorously, as though the erection of her landmark were equivalent to a pace beyond it.

It was indeed more to her taste when the land-mark was itself so outstanding that she had no need to dignify or elaborate some arbitrary point of time—as, for example, when " that Wednesday " would cease to be a day in the middle of the week (selected only for its emptiness and lack of coher-ence with the scheme of life), and would become " Miss Beeler's last go at my new dressing-gown," or " the day Lampreys promised that we should have a sample of the new note-paper." The notion of newness was bound up with that of landmarks. It would be folly to say " the day the washing has to go," and thus prolong a love-less past, although (in the later portions of the period) one might reckon that the washing would only " go " twice or once more before—and here the imagination had to be restrained. Let us call the blank simply " May the 14th."

Miss Clame had, indeed, more than once sought refuge in arithmetic. " Before May the 14th," she told herself, " I shall eat only fifty-eight meals. I shall walk in Tottenham Court Road not more than eighty-two times. I shall spend not more than five shillings in postage stamps. I shall buy but one more tube of tooth-paste and no new tooth-brush. I shall have reduced my banking account to eighty-two pounds. I shall go nine times to the cinema." But it was a dull method. The transition from fifty-eight to fifty-seven, from fifty-seven to fifty-six was meaningless. One might as well count seconds in the hope of shortening an hour.

The last of all landmarks (so near was it to the desired day) was a lunch at the invitation of Miss Gweller. (" Only four, three, two meals before I lunch with Ruth.") Gwyllyth had been pro-mised, and indeed arrived before time, chose his menu with care and had begun to consume it when the two women joined him.

"Gwyllyth is a boor," said Miss Gweller proudly.

Gwyllyth was round-faced and podgy, his sparse hair (all of which grew in a tuft on the extreme left of his head) plastered economically over the whole surface so as to afford as ample a covering as possible. His short-sightedness seemed a characteristic rather than an infirmity. The restaurant was good and quiet. Miss Clame faced a window with an oblong pane of glass above the curtain rod, and whenever she raised her eyes, as frequently she did, above the level of Gwyllyth's damp forehead, she was forced to see, through the top pane, the first-floor window of a mean house opposite. Out of this window, raised barely eighteen inches from the sill, protruded a girl's head and shoulders; though so dim was the hair that Miss Clame took the figure for that of an old hag, until a stray sunbeam revealed an anæmic gold. The watcher's right hand, containing a muddy handkerchief, was pressed so tightly against her right cheek as to seem a part of it. The fingers of the left hand picked at the grimy stone sill. The colourless eyes gazed with inflexible hopelessness into the restaurant, devouring continually those dainties which the mouth was never privileged to taste.

"Betty Green-Travers," said Miss Gweller, "is motoring to Switzerland in July—a large party, two cars, two maids and a man."

"Who is driving?" asked Miss Clame.

"Lappy, I suppose, one car, when Desmond doesn't want to. As for the other, I'm not sure: probably one of the young men of the party."

"Poulet Maryland and a double portion of maize," demanded Gwyllyth.

"Who are they?"

"I think it's not quite settled. I was asked to go."

"The young men, I meant."

"Oh, I don't know. They can afford to choose."

"I like the banana done without bread-crumbs."

"Really, Gwyllyth, we have hardly finished our *hors-d'œuvre*."

"You were late."

"I hear Mavïna is quitting you, Lydia."

"Oh no."

She quivered, looked aloft, and on meeting those absorbed eyes quivered again.

"I have often wondered which of you three would be the first to leave."

" Which one do you think would go first ? "

" I think, at all events, that you would stay till last."

" I ? Oh, surely not. I have often had thoughts of going. Besides, if one went, it would break up the flat. Two couldn't keep it up."

" Could you not find a new third ? "

" Never. It would mean the end of spin—, of living as we are. Has Mavina confided in you, or is it all second-hand ? "

" Like most people, Mavina confides in me from time to time. Gwyllyth, will you please go to the telephone and tell Lady Moore that, owing to an unparallelled headache, I cannot take tea with her this afternoon ? "

" Go yourself."

With a deft gesture Miss Gweller took Gwyllyth's crowded plate and placed it under the table. Two waiters approached in dismay, but she waved them off.

" It is of no consequence. We are but pausing," she said airily.

" Of course, you cat, if you choose to make a scene——"

" Go to the telephone, Gwyllyth."

With a heavy jerk he wrenched himself from

the table, and, treading on many toes, slouched from the room.

" Have you heard about Jenny Sale ? "

" No.　What ?　She's coming to our — I expect to see her soon."

" What is she coming to ? "

(Miss Gweller had no invitation for May the 14th.)

" To see me soon, I said.　What about her ? "

Miss Gweller's neck was squeezed by a hot hand.

" What number did you say ? "

" Look it out in the book."

" There isn't a book."

" Tell them to get you one."

" Don't you remember the number ? "

" No."

Again Gwyllyth made his baffled way to the door.　Miss Gweller bent forward until the strawberry on her hat tickled Miss Clame's nose, and whispered.　Miss Clame blushed.

" Oh, Ruth ! "

" I long suspected it."

" But in a public place ? "

" It lends a spice — to some disordered natures."

" An absolute stranger ? "

" Absolute."

" I cannot believe it."

" Gwyllyth must not hear of this. He's one of those who like things made easy for them. He has no love for conquest. He must not be led on. His virginity I rate above my own."

" It must be pathological," said Miss Clame.

" Gwyllyth ? Never ! "

" No. I was thinking of Jenny. Reggie Muswell says so."

" Indeed. And what does that youth know about it, pray ! "

" He has read *Humperdinck on the Moral Emotions*, and he has been analysed by Dr. Brancker of Prague."

" Hm ! Did he find much ? "

" Nothing at all, I believe, except that his———"

" Sh. Here's Gwyllyth. Well, Gwyllyth, did you give the message ? "

" Lady Moore was out," he said sulkily.

" Well, well. I suppose there was a butler or somebody of that sort about ? "

" I never thought of that," he mumbled. " Where's my plate ? "

Miss Gweller dived beneath the table, and produced a repulsive ruin of congealing fat.

" It looks to me," she said, " as if Lydia has been careless with her foot."

" I must have a new portion."

61

" How can we wait for that ?   I have to be in Clerkenwell by a quarter to three."

" Who asked you to wait for me ?   I'm not going to Clerkenwell."

" Waiter—*l'addizione*."

" Your pardon, Madam ? "

" The bill, as quickly as you can, please. Bring three coffees, two brandies, and a little Stilton for the gentleman—and don't forget to include them.   I am pressed for time."

" I never take brandy, Ruth."

" I know, Lydia.   I did not order one for you."

" Are you staying long in London, Mr. Gweller ? "   It was almost her first remark to him, but the Stilton's arrival prevented him from replying.   Miss Clame felt that the meal was already too long and erected a tiny landmark to help it on its way.   " I shall only look out of the window twice before we rise," she thought.

Miss Gweller spoke for her brother, while settling the account.

" He has so many invitations that he does not know ˙where to go," she said.   " If it can be managed, we shall stay with Lady Cecily towards the beginning of July, though we are promised to the Van Zwemmers during Henley.   Well, I must go this instant or I shall be late for my league meeting.   Sir Basil Verrey's car is waiting outside for me.   Can I give you a lift, Lydia ? "

She rose firmly, and Miss Clame looked yet again through the glass panel opposite.   The watcher still maintained her cramped position. " How awful it would be," thought Miss Clame, " if she were to fall out as I walked below.   But no doubt the window presses too tightly on her backbone."   She shuddered, and as, like a gambler taking in a small stake, she withdrew her fascinated gaze, she felt her own back splitting with a dull ache and colourless blood oozing from a bruised right cheek.

VIII

DEEVIE was in a strained attitude over the sky of a worthless little water-colour, when Mavina, heralded by her creaking boots, opened the door and left it open.

" I have had," she said, " the most appalling news."

Deevie gave her a look. (People made fun of one so.)

" Really ? "

" It's about Jenny Sale."

" I do not care," said Deevie, " for that young woman."

" You will when you've heard this," said Mavina. " At least you'll sympathise."

(Mavina's ill-concealed belief in mankind's propension to the altruistic emotions—see Bishop Butler's sermons *passim*—never failed to amuse her more enlightened friends, who shared the belief but did not dare to say so.)

" Let us have it all, in one long sentence."

" It is very terrible."

" Come, come, Mavina. Take a breath."

" Jenny Sale was arrested yesterday morning on a serious charge."

Deevie screamed.

" On her person were found four pairs of cotton stockings, two large table-cloths, a tea cosy of Maltese lace, four and a half yards of nun's veiling and more handkerchiefs than could be counted."

" Where did it happen ? "

" At Vollin's. She was coming out of the Oxford Street entrance, looking, I suppose, bulky to say the least, when an eagle eye from within caused her to be pounced upon. Then and there—not, of course, in the entrance—she was searched, charged, taken to the police station and remanded, or whatever they do."

" Has she bail ? "

" Who would give it ? "

" Some of her men, perhaps."

" Not they."

" Will she send round to us, then ? Really, our position is delicate. We never knew her well—I least of all. But we must prepare an attitude. We must rehearse at once. ' Jenny Sale ? ' I would say. ' Do you mean Canon Sale's charming daughter who married Tom Vandeleur ? No ? ' "

" Deevie, you are absurd."

" But, Mavina, you must realise that we have some appearances to keep up. We cannot afford to be *très liées avec* Jenny Sale, as Lydia would say. The world is very hard, Mavina. It will have thrusts for us."

" And Lydia."

" Yes, Lydia, of course. How will she take it ? Will she simply giggle, touch her dimple with the lazy finger of her left hand and say, ' One of my dearest friends is a kleptomaniac. Twice a week I take marrons glacés to her cell ' ? Or will she write a little ode for *Astarte* ? "

" At least," observed Mavina sententiously, " her embarrassment will be more mingled with pity than yours."

" But it is a sin with which I have no sympathy. I feel not the tiniest temptation to commit it. Now, had it been——"

Well-known sounds indicated that some one was mounting the stairs—not the visitor's actual footfall, but a series of vibrations transmitted along the woodwork of the building which gave warning (not always inconvenient) to the occupants of the top flat.

" That, I think, must be Lydia," said Mavina. " Shall I tell her all at once ? "

" You would enjoy," said Deevie maliciously, " to soften the blow ? "

" I will wait for her mood. It may not be Lydia, either."

It was Lydia. She laboured under many perplexities. So far, she had said nothing to her companions about the proposed reception. It should be thrown at them airily. They could take it or leave it. And there was Jenny Sale. Could Geoffrey be trusted to have forgotten her? Yet, as a bait, she had served well. " And why wasn't Ruth coming? " they would ask. Why indeed! The suspicion was unreasonable but poignant.

Without troubling to assume an air of freshness, she walked into the studio. There was a silence.

" Fancy. You're both in."

" I've just come back from the club," said Mavina.

" And I from lunch with Gwyllyth."

" Indeed, Lydia."

" Ruth was there too."

" Did she economise? "

" We had one cocktail, *hors-d'œuvre*, Poulet Maryland and the offer of an ice. By the way, you haven't fixed up anything for Wednesday, have you? "

" Of course not."

67

Miss Clame dropped her hat and gloves on to a chair and nearly sat upon them, so intent was she upon the casualness of the next sentence.

"I told you, didn't I, that I had asked a few people in for Wednesday night?"

"No. How many? Is it a party? Is it anything special?"

Embarrassing questions followed.

"Gladys Lampeter, Hilda Truthways, Daisy Peverett and Randolph Groves, Reggie Muswell and his friend something Remington, Monica Beamish, Hilton Grownlow and one or two others I can't remember. Oh, and I asked Jenny Sale, but—I can hardly believe it—Ruth Gweller told me the most odd things about her. Something to do with importuning, I gathered. She burst into tears, they say, in front of a perfect stranger and said, 'Won't you take me home?' He promptly gave her in charge. Of course she was irresponsible, neurotic, one might almost say pathol——"

"I heard it was shop-lifting," said Mavina sullenly.

"Well, perhaps that's what they call it. Anyhow, she seems to be in gaol."

"And we can therefore hardly afford to have known her."

"You might be a bourgeoise of Leeds, Deevie,

68

trying to pretend to the parson that your mother's people went to church instead of chapel."

" I'm afraid, Lydia, that you're in a rude mood this afternoon."

(It was rather hot, and Deevie, not having yet attained to the ecstasy of a real heat-wave, was developing irritability.)

" Is Ruth coming ? " asked Mavina.

" She is engaged."

" Oh. And any one else ? Anybody important ? "

" I think important people find our parties rather dull."

" You might have asked Stanley."

" Which Stanley ? "

" Stanley Dalrymple, of course."

" Oh."

" Why didn't you ? "

" He's so terribly—I don't think my friends care for him much."

They bickered for another ten minutes, and eventually Deevie hissed " Why can't I be left alone with my work ? " so suddenly that Miss Clame (barely eighteen inches from the water-colour) was nearly careless with her foot the second time that day. But there was nothing for it but to leave Deevie alone. Mavina went out to tea somewhere and Miss Clame to her own

room, hoping that her companions would behave
well at the party, not be too observant, too
advanced in their behaviour, too noticeable for
anything except their background of charm (and
thus a credit to her), and that they would help
with the arrangements more than the laws of
strict duty demanded.   But nothing mattered
very much.   It was clear that the three of them
would not be living together much longer.   But
then there was Jenny Sale.   Miss Clame wrote a
little poem to her which began in this fashion :

To J. S.

On the night of your arrest
The angels may have wept, but I
(By premonitions long oppressed)
Found relief in certainty.

Beethoven's Sonatas lay
Forlorn upon my music-stand—
From time to time I tried to play,
But your disaster numbed my hand.

The maid had gone.   The fire was low.
Outside it rained, and in the rain
The policeman walking to and fro
With every step proclaimed your (? my) pain.

It became worse and worse, and on rereading
it after writing six or seven verses, Miss Clame
decided that " The angels may have wept " was

the only good thing in the whole piece.   Then she remembered :

> " Des séraphins en pleurs
> Rêvant, l'archet aux doigts, dans le calme des fleurs
> Vaporeuses, tiraient de mourantes violes
> De blancs sanglots glissant sur l'azur des corolles—
> C'était le jour béni de ton premier baiser,"

and the good thing became bad because unoriginal.   As for the poem, it was never finished but put into a drawer with many others.

IX

It was a quarter to nine on the evening of May 14th. Miss Clame sat by her bedroom window, which looked (since the room was small) across the middle of Beam Square. Had the room been larger, it would have been a reception room, and Miss Clame's bedroom would have faced the squalor of the grim bedrooms (never uncurtained) at the back of the house.

In the garden of the square were flourishing all the usual trees and shrubs. The grass had an uneven look, faintly suggestive of a neglected park. The sunlight faded and became more watery every minute. In its calm radiance the roses in the centre bed seemed bronze. The little scene was filled with a dim tranquillity, which, seeming pastoral at first, led the thoughts irresistibly to wider spaces, to an immensity of plain or sea or sky where night and day melted together in a swoon of non-existence, and the many-sided earth itself dissolved, like a crystal falling through deep waters. For a few minutes one could be overcome, transmuted into something passive yet passionless. The quiet was premonitory of nothing, the laburnums changeless, the lilacs more perennial than stone. The loveliness of summer had crept into Beam Square, floated up through Miss Clame's open window, even though it was the window of a third-floor flat, even though the sunset was yellow rather than rose.

To Miss Clame each tree and shrub were well known. Like certain tricks of speech or modes of thought, they were part of her existence. They were, she chose to think, a reflection of her, more intimate than a portrait, more faithful than her own descriptions of herself. " People who have seen this, have seen me," she decided. " In absorbing this landscape, I have taken its character. It has an unearthly beauty. It has an immortal beauty." For a few moments she was amazed by the treasures of ecstasy to which she could attain.

Her room was very small, yet the dressing-table, which stood against a wall at right angles to the window, made a superb show. It was an old painted chest of drawers, of broken yellow edged with a dull green border from which sprouted dull red flowers. An oblong of plate glass covered the top, and supported a mirror of similar colourings, a set of brushes in pale green enamel and a few cut-glass bottles filled with attractive liquids. On either side of the mirror was an amber glass candlestick with little amber lustres. She had concentrated upon the dressing-table.

The light grew dimmer. She lit the tall yellow candles in the amber candlesticks and sat down in front of the dressing-table not without pride. " To live amongst beautiful things and beautiful people," she thought, " is surely the only ideal." Then she saw her own face reflected in the mirror, the untidy wisps of her light chestnut hair, a forehead inclined to be puckered, slightly tilted grey eyes, a delicate sensitive nose and a mouth that might be passed over as insignificant, two pinched cheeks, paler than they were to be later that evening, an over-pointed chin, a thin neck tapering down to the absence of a breast. Even the kind candle-light could not do everything.

At half-past six they had had a high tea. Then they had pulled the furniture about, prepared the room for charades or even dancing. Then Miss Clame had begun to dress, and, loitering, had been impressed by the garden in the square. Her excitement, intermittent always, left her suddenly. She was exhausted, was and looked thirty. Without vitality, how make a success of the evening, how survive it? So much, once, had seemed to depend upon that evening; yet what pleasure, after all, could it possibly give her? She had invited a varied little flock, each member selected as harmless and amusing save the one who was to be amused and yet unharmed. What did she want with this young man? He was ignorant and indifferent. Probably he would forget to come. If he came, it would be out of an odious regard for Jenny Sale. His dull wits paralysed conversation. He had eyes only for the superficial. His friends were not her friends, his standards not her standards. Hers was a lamentable folly, hardly to be confessed, a symptom of mania, pathological. She would pull herself together, take mental stock, amend her ways— meet General Osgood half-way up the stairs to the dowagers' landing. There might easily have been no one there by the banisters, no admiring smile, no affectionate hand.

She went to the window again. It was dark, but her eyes reconstructed the garden from its outline. The loveliest thing was the grass under the chestnut tree. It had just the look of a neglected park, reminded one of long avenues, formal gardens with yew hedges, fountains, statues of Cupid and Psyche, the sweet melancholy of gurgling waters or the sweeter melancholy of

75

water-lilies spreading indolent leaves amongst the reflected stars. There, when the ivy-clad clock struck the hour, Pelléas would meet Mélisande for the last time, resigned already to the coming renunciation.

For a moment, as she cast her mind into the darkness, her dryness left her. Then prudishly she thought of inquisitive eyes scanning her perhaps through chinks in the foliage, or upturned in the street, pulled the curtains and withdrew, tired and numb once more.

"For five minutes," she thought, "I will rest," and she lay down on the bed, half covered with her finery though it was. Down the passage Mavina creaked to the bathroom. In the next room Deevie was patting the cushions on the divan. Poor girl, no doubt she had her hopes. In a moment she would be tapping at the door, declaring the urgency of her ideals. She was romantic and more than usually foolish. Still, the weather had been very hot, though it became cooler every minute. It was raining.

> "Outside it rained, and in the rain
> The policeman . . ."

Of course it rained *outside*. Even in Mr. Durrant's houses the rain did not come through the roof. How padding appears in the most innocent lines.

" Come in."

It was Deevie, radiant and rather beautiful, her mouth bent with a soft voluptuousness that became her.

" Why, Lydia, aren't you ready ? " she said. " They'll be coming in a minute.   I do hope the rain doesn't put any of them off."

" I shall be ready soon," said Miss Clame shortly, and she went over to the dressing-table, feeling as if by her unresponsiveness she were tearing the petals from a rosebud.   As a feeling, it was not disagreeable.

X

MAVINA had told Deevie that she thought (and after a delay Deevie had passed it on to Miss Clame) that Geoffrey had drunk rather freely. Miss Clame had been very lavish with her drinks. They were anything but those found usually in spinsters' apartments. Miss Clame had hoped (to be very honest) that the drinks would work wonders. Afterwards she regretted them; for it would have been superb to find spontaneous that geniality which Mavina's suspicion dubbed factitious.

But he had certainly been very bright, enjoyed himself thoroughly. Certain moments stood out in Miss Clame's mind like islands which she frequently circumnavigated with her thoughts. He had been more than ready to play Adam to her Eve, quite unabashed by the serpentine chaperonage of Hilton Grownlow, and in the second charade he had been excellent as Ahasuerus unveiling Vashti. (The story had been inaccurately rendered.) Then there was the ballet, and they had all flopped down on the divan. "I love a romp "—he had said. Had he really said it? It was difficult to remember what he had said. His laugh was infectious, like that of the hero of a public-school story. (" Firmly he strode along the parapet, swinging his lacrosse-bat, his boyish infectious laugh proclaiming that all was right with the world.") This was not quite Miss Clame's style. Reggie Muswell had been wittier. Reggie Muswell was a valuable friend, disinterested yet faithful.

It must have been half-past eleven when Jenny Sale, over- and under-dressed, came into the room flaunting a brazen charm.

" Good gracious, Jenny, aren't you in quod? "

" My dear girls ! "

" Did you pinch nothing ? "

" Didn't you importune ? "

Reggie Muswell had murmured diffidently about the Vagrancy Act—a statute with which at the equity bar he had no dealings. They must all have been exalted.

" Do you mean to say there's a new scandal about me ? " she had drawled in the smart manner of a temporary lady. They told her what they knew, and she laughed loudly and carefully. Hilton Grownlow seemed to be encouraged. He had been invited in order that he might restrict Jenny's advances.

79

Then came a delightful blank of another hour or two, leading up to the *feu de joie*, the crowning glory of the evening.

" We must—must meet again," said Geoffrey, holding Miss Clame's hand, and she had been bold enough to reply, " As often as you wish."

What would Lady Cecilia have said ? What did the others think, if they were not too far gone ? Had she given herself away, after all the concealments of the earlier stages ? Did Mavina know ? Did Deevie know ? If they did, what did it matter ? The time was ripe for a disclosure. It was a magnificent evening. There are times when the unluckiest of us are blinded by fortune's sudden kindness.

" We must—must meet again." During the rainy days which filled the remainder of May and the first fortnight of June, they had met almost frequently. Perhaps the meetings were due to her devising rather than to his, but for all that they were meetings, and she never cheapened herself by giving him another direct invitation. At length, he gave one to her. " I do want to show you my new rooms. Can't you come to tea ? " She accepted for the third Thursday in June.

Partial success had by now given her a partial

tranquillity. She slept better, drew less on her imagination, was more in touch with the actual, was happy and therefore surer in her conduct. For her, it was a real affair. It was a memorable summer. When she was sixty she would look back on it with a contented smile. When she was sixty she would find trivial mementoes, a snapshot, a pressed flower, one or two poems written by her and never sent to him, one or two picture postcards sent by him to her. It was very ordinary. She was becoming exceedingly normal, less of a modern girl, revealing more and more the true Victorian that she was. But she had moods of dissatisfaction, when she longed to be larger, more violent, more sinister, a sentimental vampire.

" My thoughts," she thought, " are larger and more violent than those of ordinary people. They shrink from nothing. Why, then, are my actions so shallow? Circumstances wheel me along like a baby in a perambulator, clutching with ridiculous hands at the lamp-posts. I shall never surprise any one. On the other hand, they all think they surprise me. But I am never surprised. There is no reason to suppose that thought is less important than action, though it is less agreeable."

She would often ramble on in this strain.

It was hot again on the third Thursday in June, and the sun beat down insistently on Miss Clame's back straightened by the bus seat. She was in an objective mood, having decided to anticipate nothing. How very delightful the hot sun was. It brought out a look on people's faces, a look (one might say prudishly) of enterprise and responsiveness. The bus conductor, when he gave her fourpence change, had pressed her hand. Even the bricklayers (corduroy lovebirds on their iron perches) had an archness. Some one might write a romance of demolition —perhaps a problem play. " *Act I. Scene I. A small sunless room.* MARJORIE BEETLEMERE *gazes pensively at a small window. Her mother, wrapped in shawls, mumbles. At length a sudden ray of light strikes through the window on to* MAR-JORIE'S *saintlike face.* THE MOTHER : What is that, child ? MARJORIE, *with simple ecstasy* : It is the sun ! THE MOTHER : The sun ? Never yet has the sun entered this room. As you know, child, the only sun we get in this flat is in the little room next the bathroom. MARJORIE : It is the sun. They are pulling down the great grey building in front of us. The first slate has fallen, the first chink is made, the first ray strikes home. It is the sun (*etc.*)."

Then much later : " *Act V. Scene VI. As in*

Act I. Scene I. MARJORIE, *very weak, is sitting in a chair by the window. A thin ray of sunlight falls on her wan face. Her mother, wrapped in shawls, huddles by the fire.* THE MOTHER : It is the dim December sun. Well, child, are you to wed Ralph ? MARJORIE, *with hopelessness* : Nay, Mother. He does not love me. I have released him. THE MOTHER, *almost with heat* : What ? After his scoundrelly conduct and your shame ? MARJORIE, *wearily* : Maybe, on account of it. *Pause, then the room becomes suddenly dark.* THE MOTHER, *with a scream* : What is this ? Where is the light ? MARJORIE : They have built up the great grey building in front of us. The last slate is fixed, the last chink is filled. The sun is gone, gone, gone. It is the end. *Curtain.*"

It was an admirable symbol. Some day it should be used. Perhaps the Christmas number of *Astarte* would take it. PORTS & THLETI UTFITTE. How slovenly they were with their lettering, and what a marvellous coincidence in the next ravaged shop-front. URNIS URNIS URNIS three times. If she hadn't seen the orange brocade settee and the two easy-chairs to match (a bargain, 27 guineas), could she have filled in the blanks ? She might even have thought that a Mr. Urnis owned the shop. But a fraction of an F was still visible in the third

window, while in the second was the ghost of
HERS.

Hurry up, constable ; get on with it. (Their
whole object seemed to be to hold up the traffic,
not to speed it on its way.) Why not let us get
across before that horse-van trickles across the
road ? She hated him with passion. She peered
down vehemently. He had spots at the back of
his neck which sloped into his blue collar like a
slimy blancmange. The one at the other corner
was better. What would that indolent lady in
red satin, lolling inside a marvellous mauve
Hispano, do if some one threw a stone into her
lap ? From the bus-top the feat would be easy.
Perhaps society would take up the game. " Lady
Elizabeth Bronx scored 10 for a magnificent
bull's-eye in Pall Mall. Screams brought her
total up to 23. She was, however, outclassed
by the Honourable David Huger, who brought
down eight powerful bourgeoises in succession."
Of course, the stones would not be real. They
could be charming little boxes, that opened with
a snap, revealing a guinea inside for damages.

Motor-cars must give rise to much class
hatred. Everything that is really worth having
does. " I would give anything," thought Miss
Clame, " for an Hispano. Everything, that is,
except my affections, which are already be-

spoken." She tingled a little at the thought of the pleasure awaiting her at the end of the ride.

The old gentleman next to her nudged her with his elbow.

" Pardon," he said ; " these seats are none too big."

" No," she replied, " but as it is, you have the lion's share."

He looked at her with curiosity. " No doubt," she thought, " he takes me for an imbecile ; but I know him to be a commercial traveller from Lancashire."

" And how do you like London ? " she asked.

" Where I come from, folk aren't so talk-ative," he replied rudely, and, a vacancy occurring, changed his seat. " He fears me," thought Miss Clame. " Do I look seductive ? "

Then she alighted, took a turning in St. James's Street (" *du côté de chez Geoffrey* " as she phrased it), and rang a bell.

The door was opened by a minor official.

" Can I see Mr. Remington ? Is he at home ? "

" I think Mr. Remington's away, 'm."

" Away ? Are you sure ? I understood that he—could you find out ? "

" I'll go and see, 'm. What name shall I say, 'm ? "

" Miss Clame, C-L-A-M-E."

" Right you are, 'm. I'll be down in a jiffy."

(Had she already lost prestige? But the absurd rebuff had been more than trying.)

After a long pause, the boy reappeared.

" Mr. Remington's away, 'm," he said. " But there's a Mr. Muswell in his room, and he said he'd be very glad if you'd kindly step up."

" Is there no hope—no lift, I mean ? "

" Not in this house, 'm. They have one next door, but that's not working, I hear."

They ascended several flights of stairs, until the boy knocked with irritating vigour on a door at the end of a short but dark passage—a passage that might mean so much to a girl. Miss Clame was greeted expansively by Reggie Muswell.

" This is a great surprise, Lydia. Do sit down, and have some tea."

" I should like," she said, " a little whisky and Italian vermouth with a dash of orange bitters."

As he set to work preparing the drink, she walked round the room, as if every second must be spent in search of incriminating details. On a table were a number of big photographs. They were male groups. To these she would return at leisure. On the mantelpiece was a miniature of Lady Cecilia, and next to it a photograph of Geoffrey's sisters, plain and ungainly. An unframed photograph lay face downwards on the writing-table. She turned it over. It was signed in sprawling letters : " To G. R. in great affection —yours ever devotedly, Helen Vayadère." It was dusty and there was an ink blot on the bulging corsage, while another had only just missed the nose.

" Here you are. I haven't any orange bitters, so I put in angostura."

" Thank you. Do you live here, Reggie ? I thought your number was 34."

" So it is. It's another house belonging to these people. I've been there nearly a year and told Geoffrey about these rooms. My own room's being done up to-day—an extraordinary woman above me left the bath-tap on, and it all came through the ceiling ; she had, of course, no right of stillicide."

" What ? "

" Running of water—a legal term. So, as Geoffrey was going to be away to-day he put this at my disposal, as they say. What do you think of it ? Of course, I've got my own furniture and have had the walls redone. Still it isn't a bad room, is it ? (Mine's just the same size.) Right in the heart of bachelordom. Now, won't you let me give you some tea ? I was just going to make some for myself."

Somewhat dazed, she sank on to a settee near the groups.

" Tea would be nice," she said, and while he adjusted the electric kettle, she looked through the photographs weakly. They were chronologically arranged—Geoffrey standing at the back of a row of small boys, a little diffident, perhaps about fifteen—Geoffrey sitting in the centre of some flannelled youths, older and more important (the second XI.)—Geoffrey standing again, but it was the first XI., Geoffrey supreme in middle of them. At every stage he gained an attraction. Then there were pictures of football elevens (fifteens rather), house groups, college groups, and some rather intriguing groups of Territorial officers with Geoffrey radiating bonhomie from behind the Colonel. At that period the moustache began.

" I keep telling him to burn those things," said Reggie, without looking up. " There's nothing I hate so much as photographs more than a week old. I'm afraid Geoffrey's taste is immature."

" Do you know him well ?   Do you see much of him ? "

" No. We are so different. I am too intelligent for him. He plays cricket."

" Does he consult you, ask your advice ? "

" Never. It would be better for him if he did. Do you like cakes with puce icing ? "

" Thank you. I prefer the beige."

" I still don't understand," said Reggie vaguely —no doubt he was thinking of something irrelevant, and asked a question so as not himself to be compelled to answer one—" how you come to be here. Did you know I was in this room to-day ? "

Miss Clame looked twice at her watch. Her head was none too steady, but she realised that she had not yet met the full backwash of disappointment. Almost she revealed everything to Reggie. But she, like him, was in a dry mood. Was it worth while pursuing explanations, hoping for a clue amongst the material objects in the room, an oracle displayed in the unconscious Reggie ? To be left alone would have been admirable, to have paced up and down for ten minutes, peering through the window now and again (as if keeping an eye on an orgy in the attic opposite), taking a book from the shelves, noticing dedication and edition, turning over more photographs, to have studied the handwriting on all those random envelopes, almost to have peeped inside those envelopes. It was too easy to be clear as to the conversation that would pass between the pair of them, if once she gave the answer (to the question which he had forgotten), and said : " I came to have tea with Geoffrey." (Could the pathos be kept out of the voice ?) Over the remainder of the sequence one would have more command. (*He :* " Oh, I am sorry ; you must be disappointed." *She :* " How can I be, finding such a substitute ? " *He :* " ! ! ! Would you like to have tea with me some day ? " *She :* " Of course." *He :* " Well, then, when ? " *She :* " Almost any day, except," etc. *He :* " Then shall we say the — ? " *She :* " And at what o'clock ? ")

This could not be faced.

" Forgive me," she said, " I must go."

And Reggie, priding himself upon his adaptability to all emotional surprises, gave her a nod of comprehension and opened the door without a word.

XI

THE birds of the air (or else a squeaking that counterfeited them) enjoined her to be vernal; for, although it was mid-June the usual English monsoon had done much to preserve an illusion of spring. The grass, wherever it appeared, was not parched, and now that the sun was obscured by a cloud no bigger than a man's hand, there was a chilliness.

"I will walk," thought Miss Clame, "all the way."

"But," she continued to herself, "I wonder if I am too drunk to reach home. With every pace my dizziness increases. Positively, I do not see how I am to cross Piccadilly. One lurch and I am ground underfoot by a bus. (And the disgrace of the post-mortem! 'An examination of the organs of the deceased showed that she was in a state of acute inebriation.') Perhaps the cold air will clear my head. Perhaps, on the other hand, it will not. If I keep to the south side, I shall only have the little streets, and at the Circus I can take stock of myself once more."

She passed Hatchard's window, and looked at it for a long time, displaying, as she thought, intelligence in deciphering the titles on the books, until she found that she was pressing the glass with the thumb of either hand, as if it had turned to a bell-push beneath her touch. How often do we press things with the thumb—with both thumbs? Yet if we suffer an abrasion on any part of the body, we feel that our contact with the external world is derived entirely from that part. Lip or heel when blistered show themselves equally indispensable.

At Piccadilly Circus she wondered whether or not to take a bus. But, being at the south-west corner, she only encountered those going in the wrong direction, and the problem of crossing the road made her realise how ill she was feeling. Had she not been ill, one drink could not have undermined her. To walk the streets of London, jostled with imagined hostility and real indifference at every step, wondering whether one's weak dizziness will allow one to reach the next refuge, the shelter of the next recess in the wall, must be the lot of many. Miss Clame found herself identified in a world-tragedy that had not interested her before. The thought of it all, and the combination of her extreme feebleness with an odd lucidity of self-consciousness, pleased her a

little ; for the complexity of her sensations less-
ened their unpleasantness. Still, she felt at every
moment that in her abstract mood she might
violate one of the laws of science at a terrible
cost—forgetting, for example, to stand upright,
or misjudging the mass of her own body in relation to the mass of a motor-lorry moving at
full speed. It alarmed her to think that a trivial
action (or the momentary failure to act) might
play such havoc with her substance. She would
be safer in bed, and the next best thing to bed was
a taxi. She hailed one, hoping that her faculties
would allow her to give a coherent and correct
address to the driver. If at the journey's end
she had forgotten how to reckon the change or
the meaning of the figures on the meter, help
could be obtained.

> " Rolling home drunk of an afternoon,
>   An afternoon, an afternoon,"

she sang softly to the rhythm of the wheels, all
the way up Shaftesbury Avenue and Tottenham
Court Road, and when she reached Beam Square
she managed to enter her house like a perfect
lady.

" And now what shall I do ? " she thought.
" It seems so dull to go to bed. Shall I do the
accounts, or get on with my D'Annunzio ? Both
are within my powers."

Then an elaborate spasm swept through her—
not merely simple nausea—and she went to bed.
When her companions came in, they gave her
homely remedies. She looked at them with a
wan smile and said : " I am undergoing all the
sensations of a death." They would have spent
the night watching by her bed-side, but she sent
them away. During the night she awoke three
or four times, and then slept till eleven. When
asked if she would see the doctor, she demanded
breakfast, and ate a little of it when it came. " I
am quite well," she said, and they realised that
her trouble was not where they thought it was,
and left her.

" I must reason things out," she told herself,
and spent a few miserable hours trying to do so.

At four o'clock that afternoon she found the
supreme peace of resignation to the worst. She
was calm, and told herself that she was happy.
Being alone in the flat, she rose and made herself
some tea. Then, straying to the window as if
she were visiting it from another world, she
justified her mood with a little poetry.

> " Silvia, rimembri ancora," she read,
> " Quel tempo della tua vita mortale
>   Quando beltà splendea
>   Negli occhi tuoi ridenti e fuggitivi,

> E tu, lieta e pensosa, il limitare
> Di gioventù salivi ?
> Sonavan le quiete
> Stanze, e le vie dintorno
> Al tuo perpetuo canto . . ."

after which she had to hunt up the parallel passage
from Goethe :

> " Wie anders, Gretchen, war dir's
> Als du noch voll Unschuld
> Hier zum Altar tratst,
> Aus dem vergriffnen Büchelchen
> Gebete lalltest,
> Halb Kinderspiele,
> Halb Gott im Herzen. . . ."

Strictly speaking, the Evil Spirit's moralising
was beside the point, but the first line was most
satisfying, " Wie anders, Gretchen, war dir's . . ."
—more satisfying even than her own poems,
which she began to read aloud, having taken them
from a locked drawer in the bureau. Had she
known her FitzGerald better, she could indeed
have hit upon four lines with a peculiar reference
to herself and her poetry-reading :

> " So with Division infinite and Trill
> On would the Nightingale have warbled still,
> And all the World have listened ; but a Note
> Of sterner Import checked the love-sick Throat."

The note of sterner import was the voice
(heard many days back at Mrs. Peverett's party
and now suddenly recollected) of Princess Vaya-

dère saying, as she said good-bye to Geoffrey,
" You must come to my next Thursday "—and
as soon as the note sounded, the memory of the
photograph of the same Princess lying smudged
on Geoffrey's table came into Miss Clame's mind,
shattering the gossamer of her illusory content-
ment, and opening up another Hell yawning beneath that which she had so serenely plumbed.
There was no limit to the Princess's Thursdays,
and their attractiveness no doubt so numbed
man's senses that dates, decency and duty were
alike forgotten. Thus, in a flash, she had hit
upon the awful secret which three hours of
" reasoning things out " had failed to tell her.

" Come the third Thursday in June," he had
said to her.

" You must come to *all* my Thursdays," the
Princess had said to him.

Both had obeyed.

She put on a hat and a meagre fawn coat and
went out, walked round her own square twice,
and then to the next square round which she also
walked. From this she went to the next and then
to the next, till she had like a giant skater made
figures throughout the whole neighbourhood.
Perhaps the exercise was good for her. Mentally
she would have been as well employed exclaim-
ing " Great is Diana of the Ephesians "; for

96

she noticed nothing and thought of nothing the whole time.

When she came in, Mavina and Deevie had returned, which annoyed her. " Some one called while you were out," Mavina said. " Geoffrey Remington. He waited a little and then wrote a note for you. Here it is. I hope his epistolary style is more fluent than his conversation."

Miss Clame withdrew to her own room.

" DEAR MISS CLAME—I'm afraid you'll think me so rude that you won't even trouble to open this. I really can't apologize enough about yesterday. The fact is, I'd been suddenly asked to play for the Cobras against the Vipers— (cricket)—and I had such a rush in getting down to Whittlegrove where the match was, that everything else went clean out of my head. I am most awfully sorry, though it's lucky that Muswell was there. I have to go abroad to-morrow for some time, but I do hope you'll let me fix up something when I get back.—Yours v. sincerely,   GEOFFREY REMINGTON.

" P.S.—If you're interested you'll find a report of the match in the *Field*. I did pretty badly : took only 2 wickets, made 13 not out in the first innings and 0 in the second."

XII

DEEVIE was having a few friends to tea. They included Jenny Sale (with whom she was now on the best of terms), Hilton Grownlow, Stanley Dalrymple, Randolph Groves, Gladys Lampeter and Hilda Truthways. " A common little lot," Miss Clame had said, declining to be present.

" Is her affair heart-breaking ? " asked Hilda.

" These baby-snatchers," said Jenny Sale, " have a thin time. Why doesn't she marry Osgood and have done with it ? I would if he asked me."

" Haven't you been able to compromise him, Jenny ? "

" Pig ! "

" Lydia," said Deevie with malice, " every day gets more uppish and standoffish. That's all her affair has done for her. The man's in Paris now——"

They rocked with laughter.

" But she hopes that he's dying to get back to her."

" Detained on business in Paris ! "

" What's his job ? "

" Diplomatic, I believe. Hasn't passed yet. In fact, I think he's over age." The men snorted. (Dalrymple was something in a bank, Grownlow was once a medical student and Groves called himself an actor.)

" You know, she's only seen him half a dozen times in her life, and each time they meet he behaves as if he was being introduced to her for the first time. She thinks, poor soul, that she's being so discreet."

" Our ostriches."

" We have to pretend to know nothing."

" Meanwhile she gets thinner than ever. What you call ' atonic dyspepsia,' isn't it, Hil ? "

" H'm ! Well, it might be that—or it might be something else."

He winked, and they rocked again.

" Oh, you medicals," said Jenny, " I'm sure you'd be exciting husbands."

" Why not try one ? "

" I suppose," said Gladys, " Lydia doesn't think we're quite the goods for the future Mrs. R."

" She's having tea with Reggie Muswell."

" And what does she get out of him ? "

" Really ! " said Deevie. " I think we're being a little catty about the poor woman."

99

"I don't think she'll get much out of Muswell," said Grownlow.

"Now, Hil!"

"Does she write poetry now?" asked Jenny.

"Oh, rather, reams. It's all in that drawer."

"Oh, do let's see it."

"It's locked."

"That doesn't matter. Let me try and open it."

"I could never countenance that," said Deevie, drawing herself up in queenly fashion.

They laughed, and all begged to be allowed to try to open the locked drawer.

"Have another cocktail and say 'Yes,'" urged Dalrymple. "I'm a nib at opening things."

"Plenty of practice on the safe, eh, Stan, old man," said Groves, becoming more at home every moment.

Deevie could refuse nothing to Dalrymple.

"Promise you won't leave a mark."

"He never does."

"Like the way of an eagle, etc.," said Grownlow.

"Oh, I say, do you read Ethel M. Dell?"

The lock was a very simple one; indeed, so deft was Dalrymple that it might hardly have been a lock at all. A dozen eager hands fumbled in the drawer and passed round odd sheets of paper. In a minute every one was striking an attitude and declaiming.

" Thou art my strength, but I, alas, thy weakness :
　Thou art the blade and I the unwished bread.
　Yet charity finds food awhile in meekness,
　And scorn crowns ashenly the proudest head. . . ."

" Fairer than roses when the flames of June
　Have kindled them to scented ecstasy,
　Fairer than cadence of an Indian tune
　Or the smooth cream of African ivory,
　Fairer than . . ."

" Hope, strength, despair and pain—these are to me
　The many-winged precursors of my fate,
　Voluble heralds ushering in the state
　Of my new love's refulgent royalty. . . ."

" I that have loved and lived to you that live
　But love not . . ."

" To J. S.

" On the night of your arrest
　The angels may have wept, but I
　(By premonitions long oppressed)
　Found relief in certainty. . . ."

" Who's J. S. ? " asked Grownlow, into whose hands the last fragment had come. " It must be you, Jenny ! "

" Indeed," said Jenny. " Have I inspired her wretched muse ? "

101

" Now that I come to think of it," said Gladys, " we never really got to the bottom of your escapade, Jenny. What was it really ? "

" My escapade ? Which one ? "

More laughter, far from silent, tittered round the place.

" Lydia said," remarked Deevie unpleasantly, " that you asked a perfect stranger to take you home."

" My God, of all the foul-minded creatures ! I'll teach her to say things like that."

She was so inflated with anger that she seemed about to burst. Deevie was alarmed and felt that she had gone too far.

" It was only something another of your friends told her," she said, " and she only repeated it to us."

" I seem to have a fine lot of friends," said Jenny.

" Never mind," Grownlow reassured her. " You've got me, you know." And he gave her a squeeze.

" Now, don't you think we might put them back," said Deevie, eyeing anxiously the door, as if there might enter through it at any minute the friend whose foibles she had so scandalously laid bare.

" I've a good mind," said Jenny, " to put a toad in as well."

Fortunately there was no toad to hand.

Then they drank a little more, danced, acted charades and drifted away in small groups. When they had all got clear of the square, Stanley Dalrymple turned back and re-entered the house. In his absence, Deevie's mood had altered. She became yielding and slightly convulsive, while he was the strong man in tender vein. If she could have avoided being kittenish, it would have been a very gallant scene.

Meanwhile Miss Clame was walking home.

For some days, she had told herself that she must cultivate Reggie Muswell. As she herself changed, her companions changed too. Mavina was all right—Deevie was impossible, while words could not describe the awfulness of Deevie's friends. Gulfs appeared on all sides ; tastes, habits and even accents became separated by deepening chasms. Slowly but surely she must forsake the old paths. At first, during the novelty of emancipation from Aunt Dawes, the communism of Beam Square had been amusing. People who disapproved were called " sticks " or " prudes " or even " snobs ". But as one grew older—no, as life developed—one became more conscious of one's position. After all, she was born in a different world—daughter of an army

man. She had her friends still in that world—
above it, some of them. The Homfrays, the
Peveretts, the Gwellers, the Brownes, and—
might one add ?—the Remingtons were of another stratum. Gently Deevie must be shown.
. . . Perhaps she had been shown ; for she had
been exceedingly peevish for some days. Of
course it was difficult ; as Miss Clame had somewhat rashly aped the duchess in declaring that
class distinctions were only significant to bourgeoises from Leeds, and it became clear that a
little recantation was necessary. Still, one could
make excuses. " I don't care who their people
were ; I don't care what their jobs are. Ordinary
social distinctions mean nothing to me. But I
simply can't stand people with bad manners and
common voices." (For three days past she had
gone about detecting commonness in people's
voices.)

Reggie Muswell was all right. He was a nice
youth. He had some charming acquaintances.
The need for sympathy and self-revelation had
driven her to him. She had hoped for a very
intimate tea. " The way I feel for Geoffrey . . ."
she would have liked to say, and he should have
replied, " I can see through his reserve. He's
terribly shy, but you mustn't think he lacks
feeling." " Do you ever feel like that ? " they

would have asked one another. " If it was hopeless, I should advise you to give it up ; but, really, I think that when he comes out of his shell, etc."

Unfortunately, conversation at tea had not taken this turn. It was a pity, because she had lavished several excellent remarks upon his unresponsiveness. " One passes," she had said, " two-sevenths of one's life asleep, two-sevenths doing mechanical or menial work, one-seventh feeling physically ill, one-seventh being worried, and of the remaining seventh three-quarters being bored, one-sixteenth . . ." " Please," he had interrupted. " I can never follow fractions. It's like a will case—one-twenty-first part of my residue to Jane Smith if she marries before attaining thirty-five, with the addition of two-ninths of the eleventh share of my uncle's estate to which I am entitled by virtue of an indenture of settlement dated, etc. . . ."—and her amazing analysis of the last four hundred and forty-eighth part of life had to be undisclosed.

" The sin against the Holy Ghost," she had said, " is missing an opportunity." " Moral progress is self-emancipation from the taboos of the so-called moral law." " We all have many personalities, but the more we cultivate fine and dangerous emotions the more we discover which ones we desire to make part of our true selves." " So far from my emotions being reduced to the level of sensations, I can now never experience a sensation without its setting up a current of emotion in me so violent as to be almost overwhelming." " Perhaps you have noticed that during the last three months I have undergone a stupendous change ? "

He had listened with a look of lavish attention that he bestowed—or would some day bestow—upon important solicitors whom he failed to understand. And then he had suggested a tune on his gramophone. He had played a Debussy song sung by Mme. Edvina, and when she had asked for the quintet from *Meistersinger* he had said that it would be impossible at any concert to have Mme. Edvina and the artists who sang the quintet together. She had not understood at first, but learnt afterwards that he imagined himself to be an impresario engaging the singers and conductors, and that a performance of a drawing-room Ballad after the Prelude to *Tristan* would have appeared to him not a piece of musical impertinence, but a technical impossibility. " You must realise," he had said, " that this is a big gala at the Albert Hall. Obviously only Chaliapin can come now, and very fortunate we are to have his services."

" So that is why," thought Miss Clame, " the owners of gramophones will never play you what you want. They are only interested in programme - making." Reggie's unwillingness to oblige did not encourage confidences, and it was with some coldness that she said good - bye. About Geoffrey she had learnt nothing, except that when he returned from Paris he was going straight to Moulton Bassett to celebrate a birthday—his twenty-sixth?—in the bosom of his family. Miss Gweller would be there.

This news was not particularly agreeable, and Miss Clame's meditations were sour, to say the least, when she ascended the interminable stairs leading to the flat and found Deevie twinkling like a Christmas tree.

" Oh, Lydia," exclaimed Deevie (the recent baseness of her nature transmuted into a radiant gold), " I have a great secret to tell you. Can you guess ? "

" I suppose you're engaged again," said Miss Clame pettishly, " to somebody like your Dalrymple. Is that it ? "

" Yes," and she turned away crestfallen.

" Oh. Well, of course, I wish you happiness. Had he to lock the door when he proposed ? "

After this, the two women disliked one another without interruption.

XIII

AUGUST (symbolising the future) and all its problems, like ribald waves swirling against a sand-castle, drew nearer. Deevie, not content with breaking up what they all insisted upon calling " our *ménage à trois* ", became increasingly irritating. For a day and a half she had gone about singing :

> " General Osgood
> Really was good,"

and thus forcing Miss Clame to envisage a disagreeable remedy, which she preferred to keep locked up, as it were, in a medicine-chest of the subconscious rather than let it replace the Sèvres ornament on the mantelpiece of her conscious life. Deevie's loss would be a blessing, though it would be a struggle to maintain the flat with Mavina. Then there were wisps of evil gossip floating from Paris and Moulton Bassett. In Paris what entanglements were not suggested— night clubs, cabarets, and worse, the details left to Miss Clame's too lively imagination ? At

Moulton Bassett there was Miss Gweller, and the sinister Miss Gweller, in spite of her forty years and grim figure, seemed to have no limit to her powers. When Geoffrey's engagement to her was rumoured, they had all said, " Impossible! Ruth Gweller? He must be one of those men who don't care for women. (There are a good many like that nowadays.)" But time lent credibility to the tale, and the next rumour, that Geoffrey had proposed but had been rejected, was only half encouraging.

" Must I, then," thought Miss Clame, " make myself as ugly as I can, to please his perverse fancy? Have all my face-massages, my undulations, transformations, bobbings and shinglings been in vain? Is one severe black velveteen more profitable than all my laboured wardrobe? Perhaps all along he has taken me for ugly, and would have been still more drawn towards me had I not in my silliness done my best to neutralise that sorry charm."

Almost less formidable his cult of Betty Green-Travers and Princess Vayadère. At least, one's normal instincts would help one to compete with them, whereas this *misère* was a game played too much in the dark. It was hard to credit Geoffrey with so unsavoury an asceticism. More credible, though not very reassuring, was the intelligence that he had gone from Moulton Bassett to join the Green-Travers in Switzerland. No doubt he drove one of their many motor-cars. Miss Clame pictured intimacies among the edelweiss and compromising games of "Hunt the Chamois". " In Swiss chalets," Deevie told her, " all rooms communicate." " I think the Green-Travers will not stray far from the best hotels," she had answered, painfully aware that the " younger members of a party " are never content unless engaged on some half-clandestine uncomfortable expedition.

From Switzerland he sent her a postcard displaying a bunch of gentians tied up in pink ribbon, and encircled by the letters of LES MEIL-LEURS VŒUX, each one in a swallow's mouth. The picture reminded Mavina (who could not help seeing it, since it was she who found it in the brass-wire letter-box) of a notice in a Swiss hotel fronting the lake of Geneva : *Mm. les voyageurs sont instamment priés de ne pas encourager les mouettes en vue de la propreté de la façade de l'hôtel.*

" What does he say ? " said Miss Clame disinterestedly, when Mavina delivered her reminiscence and handed over the card. But Mavina, tactful despite the heaviness of her boots, allowed Miss Clame to read it at leisure.

"Montreux, *July* 18*th*.

" Having splendid time and done fair amount of climbing. Fine run yesterday from X—— here. Expect to be here about three weeks. Lost 42 francs in Casino at Boule last night. Putrid game. Best wishes. G. R."

" So there is nothing for it but to wait once more," thought Miss Clame, " to get through the remainder of this month, August and September as best I can, and to wait for the winter— that season of dwindling days and cooling passions —when I shall be in a smaller flat, perhaps, with hardly room for a charade and none for a dance."

The domestic question became harassing. Should she bully Mavina into retaining the Beam Square flat (which if shared by two only would involve hideous economies), or should she reconcile herself once more to the horrors of searching for a home ? Her old encounters with supercilious house-agents occurred to her. " In this neighbourhood, Modom, we have nothing less than four hundred a year." " Even in Chelsea, Modom, you will find nothing unless you are prepared to pay a premium." " We have something that should suit you exactly, Modom. Only twenty minutes from Baker Street (handy for Wembley), one large reception room, ten feet by eight, one bedroom and use of bath. Hot water ten shillings a week extra. No premium. Rent only two hundred and forty a year plus a proportion of the rates, say sixty pounds. No, there is no lift, and the bedroom receives no daylight. On the other hand, there is a quite good north window in the reception room, and the street is nearly twenty feet broad at that point."

Then there was all the expense of a removal, the breakage of precious possessions, the physical discomfort of adjusting oneself to new surroundings, the waste of nervous energy. Better live as a pauper in Beam Square. It was a pity that Mavina would not speak out and declare her opinion, but she went away to some mysterious place in the country, saying nothing but " We must think it over very carefully."

Waiting was weary work, with both Mavina and Deevie away. London was emptying itself of Miss Clame's friends—more by chance than because the season was ending. The weather became very hot, but heat was no longer a thrilling novelty. In her emotions Miss Clame had a period of barren dryness, such as saints are said not infrequently to undergo—not because their faith wavers, but because their devotional exercises fail to give them that ecstasy which has previously consoled them for the sacrifice of all mundane joys. In this mood (one of the Devil's subtlest snares for the faithful soul) temptations abound and resistance is small. Unfortunately, no one troubled to tempt Miss Clame.

Most of her time she spent indoors, rediscovering the conveniences of her flat, doting on the garden, writing a mystical epic called " The Death of the Worm ", and reading Saint-Simon's memoirs. She longed for a shaking, but nothing shook her. She longed for her character and appearance to change, but nothing changed them. She began to evolve great schemes for the transmutation of her whole personality, to devise experiences after which " one would never be the same again ". Would it not be worth while, she wondered, to spend a year in Iceland, to explore Thibet ? (" Miss Clame, the world-famed explorer of the East, will lecture to-night at the Albert Hall on her experiences in Lhassa. . . ." " One of my feet was in a crocodile's mouth, the High Priest held me by the hair, my hands were manacled and a poisonous snake was coiled round my wrist. . . .") How convenient it would have been to be married at that time ! She did once begin a letter to General Osgood, but a revulsion of feeling caused her to tear it up. The old man could not have much more than eight hundred a year, and after the first excitement of marriage (which with such a partner would not be very considerable), life would be more humdrum than ever. Eight hundred a year was a ridiculous income. So was five hundred. One should either have five thousand—or nothing at all.

XIV

PEACE COTTAGE,
                                        HELMBY VALE,
                                        LINCOLNSHIRE.

" DEAREST LYDD—Many thanks for yours.
I'm sorry you find life so boring. It's the silly
season, I suppose. I think, too—and this is the
point of my letter—that London's a silly town to
live in. Its effect on one is shattering in the end ;
at least, it is on me. I've certainly been very
happy with you and Deevie, but, as I dare say
you know, I never regarded myself as *settled* in
Beam Square. The prospect of premature old
age there is too dismal. Imagine what it
would be to grow into a typical London
spinster, every year more ridiculous through
one's economies. Old age, in London, requires
money to support it ; one must end as the *grande
dame* or nothing.

" In the country it's different. The fact is,
I've been given the offer of a job on a farm here,
and I accepted it last night. I hope you won't
think me awfully inconsiderate. The woman

who runs the place is a friend of one of my aunts
—rather advanced and all that, and in fact has
surrounded herself with quite a little colony of
pleasant people. Things won't be too rustic
really, though, of course, I can stand a good deal
of rusticity, as you know. Any way, the life
will be healthy. I'll tell you more about my
prospects when I know more. Naturally, they
aren't very grand to start with.

"I suppose you'll be getting rid of the flat.
I hope it won't be too much of a wrench for you.
If there's any of my furniture you would care to
buy—I don't suppose there is—please say so,
as I'd far rather you had it than any one. I had
thought of letting Heeton's put it up to auction.
I want a little capital, and shall be living at the
farm, which is of course furnished.

"A card from Deevie this morning. 'The
great day,' she says, 'is to be September 25th.'
Another expense! Do you think it would do if
we shared the tea set we saw in Goode's window?
As for you, Lydd, I wonder what you'll do.
Perhaps something very delightful will happen
soon. You know what I mean. Forgive this
reference to it. I shall be writing to you pretty
often about my arrangements. Cheer up.—
Best love,

"Mavina, the Cow-girl."

" *July 23rd*, 192–.   VASLEDON MANOR,
                                              VASLEDON,
                                        NR. CHELMSFORD.

" DEAR MISS CLAME—I have now prepared
the statement of your income derived from your
late father's estate for the half-year ended June
30th, and send the same herewith for your approval.
I regret to say that your income is £74, 9s. 8d.
less than it was for the corresponding period last
year, owing to the failure of Hipswell & Holtby,
Ltd., to declare a dividend on their ordinary
capital.

" Your late father in his will, after providing
that his trustees might retain his property in its
then state of investment, inserted an extraordinary
and highly irregular clause to the effect that after
your attainment of the age of twenty-five years
(when, for practical purposes, you came of age),
no investment then subsisting might be varied
without your express direction to do so.   As you
know, I did not become a trustee of your father's
estate until your twenty-sixth year, and my first
action was to advise you strongly to give us your
direction to sell these ordinary shares in Hipswell
& Holtby and to permit us to invest the proceeds of such sale in some security authorised by
the Trustee Act, 1893, or the Colonial Stock Act
of 1900.   I pointed out to you not once but many

times how speculative and dangerous was the nature of these shares, and how prudence demanded that you should sacrifice a small portion of your income in order to guard against a far severer loss in the future. I remarked also that this loss would extend not only to income but also to your capital, and expressed regret that my predecessors had not thought fit to make the exchange while the power to do so was still vested in them. In your replies you gave vent to the highly improper sentiment, to the effect (if I remember aright) that youth was the time when money was most enjoyable and that old age should fend for itself. You instanced also the fluctuations in the value of Government securities and talked (if you will pardon the phrase) some preposterous nonsense about 'policies of inflation' and the decline in certain foreign currencies being a lesson to all old fogeys who clung to low but fixed rates of interest. How far these 'modern' economic doctrines have led you (and others) astray I leave you to find out. It is sufficient for me to say that, in the last three years, gilt-edged securities have appreciated by no less than 15 per cent, while your shares in Hipswell & Holtby, which only a year ago stood at forty-two shillings a share, are now changing hands on the Stock Exchange at eight shillings and ninepence.

I do not, of course, pretend that any investment, especially in these disquieting days, is assured beyond the possibility of doubt, but it should be clear to the meanest intelligence that there is a world of difference between the safety attaching to an investment bearing the guarantee of His Majesty's Government and that attaching to an ordinary share in a small industrial company, and that to aim at safety is the first duty of a spinster without expectations.

" If you now care to authorise me to sell these shares and to reinvest the proceeds, I will of course do so gladly ; but I fear it is a case of bolting the stable door after the horse has gone. I may say that my co-trustee, Major Harvard, endorses all the foregoing remarks.

" Trusting that the deficiency which I have explained will not cause you too serious an embarrassment, and that you are well in health.—I am, Yours v. truly,

" WM. SPROLLIFORTH DIGBY."

" *Sunday*.

ELFINDALE,
GAVIN'S REACH,
NR. MAIDENHEAD.

" DEAR LYDIA—How are you ? It is quite an age since we have seen you or heard of you. It must be very hot in London at present, though you are probably too busy with festivities to notice it.

" My husband and I should be so glad if you could come to us next Friday for a few days. I'm afraid we shall be very quiet, as Wilfred has something the matter with his leg—gout, I fear— and almost all our neighbours are away. Still, you may enjoy sitting in the garden and reading and perhaps even having a bathe from time to time. The river should be a respectable temperature by now.

" The 3.32 is an excellent train from Paddington. If you are able to come, Tiffin will meet you at Maidenhead station.—Hoping so much to see you, Yours v. sincerely,

" ADELINA HOMFRAY."

XV

It was sultry and close when Miss Clame got into the train at Paddington, and as the open country appeared the sky darkened more and more every moment. For the first time in her life she admitted that she was overcome by the heat—she who had always said, " I worship the sun. Your bracing northern air makes me feel ill. Give me parrokeets flying about amongst tropical foliage ! " It is only fair to say that in addition to the heat she was troubled by seven or eight different worries, each of which could if single have been laughed away, but when in combination with the others appeared mountainous and oppressive, and produced a slight sensation of physical nausea.

At Slough she closed the windows. At the Dolphin signal - box she was suffocated, and opened them again. *Quaesivit lucem ingemuitque reperta*, as she reminded herself in a desperate outburst of classicism. What could she do, she wondered, to steady her nerves ? Take to stamp-collecting ? Was that why Gwyllyth was so bovine ? " O to be a Gwyllyth now the end is near," she said, parodying Browning out of all recognition.

At Maidenhead she collected her luggage and found Tiffin. As she walked into the station yard an immense drop of rain, falling vertically from a coal-black sky, struck her on the nose.

" Oh, Tiffin," she said, " do you think we shall get back before the storm ? "

" I hope so, Miss, indeed," he replied.

As the car entered a dark wood, there was a blinding flash, and a violent tearing sound penetrated even the murmur of the machinery. " Oh, God," she thought, remembering a paragraph in the evening paper in which " Weatherwise " had said : " The town-dweller is ten times as safe in a thunderstorm as his country cousin. High buildings, steeples and towers are a great protection against lightning. . . . In the country, to shelter amongst trees is often to walk into a veritable death-trap." She recalled also another gossipy phrase : " The neighbourhood of Maidenhead, famous for cloud-bursts and the violence of its thunderstorms."

There was another flash. " One, two, three, four, fi——" counted Miss Clame, horrified to realise that the storm was so near. Could nothing be done ? " Oh, God." Again, " Oh, God."

" From battle, murder and sudden death, O
Lord, deliver us." She recanted unashamedly.
Whatever she had said, sudden death was the
most terrible death of all. Would the trees
never end, never end ? " Faster, Tiffin," she
wailed, as though he could hear. " One, two,
three, four, five, six, seven, eight—one, two,
thr—, one, two, three, four, fi—— Oh——"
and she screamed as if she had received an electric
shock herself ; for there was a stupefying flash
and a roar, and a tree by the edge of the road
snapped through the middle and flung a great
slice of its trunk into the wood.

Tiffin applied the brakes, got out and opened
the door, finding his charge weeping hysterically
against the bedford-cord cushions.

" Are you afeard, Miss ? " he asked.

" Go on, go on," she cried, " it is death to
wait here."

They drove on. " From battle, murder and
sudden death, Good Lord, deliver us." Even
murder would be better. It would be less in-
human. How thoughtless of the Homfrays to
invite her to come at the risk of her life, not to
have warned her against the perils of their dis-
trict, not to have arranged for her to wait in a
cellar in Maidenhead. At least, Mrs. Homfray
might have come to meet her. The feeling of

powerlessness was unbearable, worse than any physical agony. If she were suffering from a fatal disease, she could bear it ; but in the prime of life, the prime of life. . . . One, two, three, four, five, six, seven, eight, nine, ten, eleven, twelve, thirt— ; (better). One, two, three, f—— Was there no peace, no rest for her ? First one trial shattered her, then another. During the last month everything had gone wrong. The universe crumbled. " I am not what I was," she thought, " I am not what I was." She looked back with envy upon herself as she was in April and May, her witticisms, her self-confidence, her airy impertinence to life. Why had she been plucked out of the circle of her friends, selected, as it were, to undergo the vehemence of new passions, assaults of evil fortune ? She was unfitted to bear such stresses. It was unfair of fate to single her out. Why could she not live as a butterfly lives the life of her butterfly group ? Yet even butterflies die, and die alone.

" Ayant peur de mourir lorsque je couche seul."

They were now out of the wood, and the storm had abated somewhat, or Miss Clame could not have raised the quotation. She was calmer, and ashamed of her lack of self-control. But she had a new fear—the fear of her own self revealed in weakness. "I am not what I was," she thought again, more reflectively. To what was she degenerating? Her collapse was an insult to her spirituality. This extreme sensitiveness, of which one is so proud, can play one nasty tricks. From her humiliation before Tiffin she would never recover. How they would relish it in the servants' hall. They would leer at her in the passage, drop tin trays beneath her window to awaken her with a start, play practical jokes with the barometer. (Henceforward, she disliked Tiffin and all the staff at Elfindale.)

When they reached the house, the rain was stopping. But the mud of the drive almost foamed beneath the wheels of the motor, and the overhanging branches dripped as though they were water-pipes. The gutters dripped round the house, and there was a big pool by the front door. There was a sweet fresh smell in the air, and Miss Clame felt invigorated, as if she had had a bath.

Mrs. Homfray, the maid said, was lying down with a headache, and begged to be excused. Mr. Homfray was resting his leg and (confidentially) asleep in the study. Miss Dorlip had gone for a walk shortly after lunch and had not yet come back. It was to be hoped that she had found some shelter.

Miss Clame was shown to her bedroom—the bedroom which she had had before. The same pink cretonne curtains turned the room into the bedroom of a doll's-house. The same pretty and inadequate wash-stand nestled in an angle of the wall. The wardrobe door creaked when one opened it. (It was not the best spare bedroom.) The furniture reminded her of those advertisements which one sees in the papers, of newly married couples setting up house together and buying their requirements on the hire-purchase system with great ingenuousness and pleasure. The young man is dashing, well dressed and eager to " make good ". He is also absurdly proud of his blushing little bride in her neat serviceable ready-made frock. Sometimes she is shown rather indelicately in bed with a fat baby nestling beside her, and the husband sitting by her feet. Sometimes baby is given a special inset complete with the perambulator which may be ordered on the same generous terms. It was a comforting thought, and Miss Clame, sitting down on her own bed, made the most of it. Perhaps, after all, she was really born to be suburban. There was much to be said for life in a small way, simple ambitions, a fair amount of hard work and just enough pleasure to keep one working for more. Such people would never disgrace themselves by screaming at a lightning flash. But, then, how little they knew. Miss Clame thought of all her own accomplishments with mingled pride and anxiety. What profited her all the literatures at her command, her patchwork knowledge of society, her moral freedom, the boldness of her imagination? It is the tallest tree which is first struck by the thunderbolt.

To still an unpleasant memory, she opened her bag and took out a pack of patience cards, and played on the writing-table in her bedroom till the bell sounded for tea.

XVI

Miss Dorlip came in shortly before dinner. During the storm she had taken refuge in Humble-bird Church, which was almost immediately struck by lightning. Miss Dorlip, however, who knew that the chance of being killed in this manner was one to nine million, was not at all dismayed, and spent an instructive ten minutes estimating the cost of repairing the damaged portion. She then walked about a quarter of a mile to the big girls' school presided over by her friend Miss Eastgate, who saw to the drying of her garments. She was thus enabled to return to Elfindale as little damaged as when she left it. She recounted her adventures in a matter-of-fact way which much displeased Miss Clame.

"I trust," said Mr. Homfray, lying on the sofa after dinner, "that the beautiful stained glass in the church was unhurt."

"It was broken into several pieces," answered Miss Dorlip. "I gathered them together and put them into collecting-bags on the altar, and wrote out a label so as to inform the authorities."

" How admirable you are," said Miss Clame.

" One could hardly have done less."

" Miss Clame, too, had an unpleasant experience while motoring through a wood," said Mr. Homfray.

" Please, don't let us speak of it again. My behaviour was feeble."

" Are you neurotic ? " asked Miss Dorlip.

" I am, I think, a little overstrung."

" One of my nieces is much affected by thunder. Her doctor has ordered her a special pill to alleviate the strain—two to be taken half-an-hour before the storm's onset. But I tell the girl that self-control is better than physic."

" Miss Dorlip is a great organiser," explained Mrs. Homfray.

" I am much interested," said Miss Dorlip, " in many Women's Movements. At the invitation of my friend Miss Eastgate (principal of St. Gradimir's College for Girls), I am delivering six lectures to the elder pupils on ' Race and Race-control.' I am also paying visits of inspection to all the Women's Institutes in this neighbourhood, for the benefit of the Central Committee. Mrs. Homfray, who is President of the Humble-bird and Hailby Institute, is kindly putting me up while I am in the locality."

" I assure you, Miss Dorlip, we take it as a

great privilege," said Mr. Homfray. "By the way, Miss Clame, did you say that you were at a loose end as to where to live next October? Miss Dorlip has an idea that might suit you."

"Oh, and what is that?" asked Miss Clame ungraciously.

"We have bought a large building," answered Miss Dorlip, "in an excellent position in North London—at the upper end of Archway Road, to be exact. We propose to convert it into a hundred bed-sitting-rooms complete with hot and cold water, a big refectory, a library, a lecture-room, and a common-room. It is designed for spinsters of slender incomes who wish to lead a fuller life than that of the semi-detached suburban villa or the two-roomed flat in West Kensington. In our establishment they will find agreeable companionship, a liberal, wholesome diet, and every incentive to take up some useful work instead of wasting their time in snatching at pleasures beyond their reach. Three times a week lectures (which all will be expected to attend) will be given on important subjects of the day. There are a few salutary restrictions—all lights out at 10.30 P.M., unless special leave is obtained, no cards, alcohol, or tobacco allowed, and an enlightened censorship of all literature brought into the building. All extravagance in dress or

personal luxury will be discouraged. Meals will
be taken in common, in the refectory—breakfast,
8 A.M., dinner, 1 P.M., and supper at 7 P.M. The
staff will make the beds, turn out the rooms once
a fortnight, do the cooking and the waiting.
Light dusting and other minor tasks are left for
the occupants. The inclusive charge, with a
fair allowance for washing, is two hundred and
seventeen pounds a year. We open on October
the 15th, and have already received over three
hundred applications. We intend to select our
nucleus with great care, so as to set the right tone
from the very first. If you care to give me par-
ticulars of yourself, I shall be happy to take them
down, though, of course, I can promise nothing."

"I fear," said Miss Clame, "that as an inmate
I should be recalcitrant."

"The old Eve, eh?" said Mr. Homfray,
wagging his forefinger.

"There is nothing," continued Miss Clame
aggressively, "which I dislike so much as communism or co-operation."

"Then I'm afraid you are old-fashioned in
your views. The whole trend of modern life is
away from wasteful individualism towards a
group-activity."

"In fact," said Miss Clame, who had read four
books on anthropology, "you revert to the

spirit of the herd, which punished originality with death. Your philosophy I find unsatisfying. I still cling to good old nineteenth-century radicalism, casting overboard, of course, the absurd moral conventions which perpetually hampered its arguments. If individualism is crushed, I shall hardly trouble to exist. I am nothing if not an individual."

" We seem to be a little polemical," said Mr. Homfray. " What do you say to a game of bridge ? "

" I never play for more than a penny a hundred," Miss Dorlip warned him.

" And I never play for less than five shillings," said Miss Clame untruthfully, like a spoilt child.

" Well, well. We seem to be at a dead-lock. Take my wife as partner, Miss Clame, and I will play against you at five shillings, while the other two can play at a penny."

" If Miss Dorlip will rise to a shilling, I will come down to that," Miss Clame suggested.

" My principles are not mere whims," said Miss Dorlip. " I never vary them to suit my company."

" Well, then," said Mr. Homfray, " we will play as I proposed. My wife and Miss Clame play against Miss Dorlip and myself. If we lose, Miss Dorlip pays my wife at the rate of one penny a hundred, while I pay Miss Clame at the rate of five shillings—and *vice versa*."

"Perhaps Miss Dorlip does not care to take part in a game in which some of the players outrage her principles?" Mrs. Homfray inquired.

"I am trusting," said Miss Dorlip with an evil glance at the clock, "that by eleven o'clock Miss Clame will see the folly of her ways."

At the end of the third rubber, the clock struck eleven. Miss Dorlip rose, and said, "I trust you will excuse me. I go to bed at eleven. Good-night." And after picking up one shilling and fourpence which Mrs. Homfray placed on the table, she left the room. Miss Clame had, through her bravado, lost four pounds, and had not even the satisfaction of dazzling Miss Dorlip by the nonchalance with which she wrote her cheque.

Why ever had the Homfrays invited her with Miss Dorlip, she wondered, as she undressed. Did they think she needed the force of such an example? She did not remember ever meeting a woman who caused her to bridle so much, a woman so far removed from romance, fantasy, caprice—"everything, in fact, that I stand for," she said aloud. If only Mr. Homfray would assault Miss Dorlip in the night. As far as Miss

Clame was concerned, screams would be of no
avail. She would even hold the door of Mrs.
Homfray's room, though interference from that
lazy quarter was unlikely. Mr. Homfray was
indeed the mildest and most ordinary of men.
"But we are all prone to strange impulses,"
thought Miss Clame hopefully.

Oh, to have Mavina, Deevie, Jenny Sale, even
Princess Vayadère at hand, to help her to maintain her own atmosphere. It was hateful to be
overridden at every turn. And four pounds was
a large sum—far more than she could now afford.
(The word "now" used in this connection
brought tears to her eyes.) Some day she would
give a cock-tail party—some Sunday afternoon
—and when they had had about six each, they
would take a taxi to Archway Road and invade
the precious institute.

"We wish to see the pr-r-r-incipal," she would
say ; "we insist on seeing the pr-r-incipal of this
establishment. . . . Is that Miss Dor-r-r-lip ? "
(It was all on the lines of "Gr-r-rosvenor two-
thr-r-ee fife foer.") Then they would make out-
rageous proposals to the pr-r-r-incipal, ask if she
had a room to let for a baccarat party, a vodka
party, an absinthe party (and worse), march into
the refectory, smash the crockery, upset the
abominable books in the library ("Labour Statis-

tics of Czecho-slovakia, 1824–1828," "The Place of Woman in Education", "Sanitary Systems of the Middle Ages "), and leave behind shilling shockers from the Vampire Press, Rio de Janiero. Really, if Miss Dorlip represented culture, culture must go, progress must go, civilisation must go. But surely real culture is the acquisition of new means of self-indulgence— the power to enhance physical pleasures by blinding them with mental pleasures—a training of the hedonistic palate to detect rare flavours ?

She became frenziedly didactic, elaborating theories at the rate of two a minute, as she sat on the bed half undressed, hot and palpitating. Then there was a sound at her door, and she thought for one minute that Mr. Homfray's " impulse " had led him to the wrong room. She was, she reflected, in no state to receive nocturnal visitors. She was wasting too much nervous energy, and had too small a store of it, as it was. The sound was not repeated, and she concluded regretfully that it must only have been a ghost or a rat.

Having flung off the remainder of her clothes and quieted herself somewhat by brushing her teeth with great care—" brushing the teeth should always be a *conscious* act," her dentist used to say—she went to the window and drew back the curtains.   Far off on the horizon she saw the flare of huge bonfires burning steadily, and remembered that she had heard at dinner that hundreds of cattle had been killed on account of the foot-and-mouth disease, and were being cremated that night.   She watched the funeral pyres for nearly ten minutes, fascinated and wondering if they had any message for her. But if they had, she was not able to fathom it, and with a little shudder she turned to bed.

XVII

WHEN Miss Clame descended next morning, she found to her relief that Miss Dorlip was out and would remain out till nightfall. " Some silly piece of officiousness," thought Miss Clame, still bitter. She had forgotten about the lectures on " Race and Race-control." Country air always made her feel dazed at first, and her thoughts were more jerky than usual.

She went out into the garden, which was quite alluring in the brilliant sunshine. In a secluded corner there was an undersized croquet lawn, and mallets and balls were available in a tumble-down rustic summer-house with thatched roof. " What a place for gallant encounters," she thought as she went inside ; for she intended to try her skill at the game.

The lawn was only slightly damp in spite of the recent rain, but some parts, as she found by experiment, were faster than others. " Can I get round in 30 ? " she wondered, making an execrable shot for the first hoop. She started again, and again, and finally completed the round in 34 strokes. She pencilled the result on a Salvation Army pamphlet which she had been given in London, and began again after some more false starts. For the next three rounds her scores were 34, 33, and 36. "I will do it in 30," she said with firmness, and went round repeatedly, becoming more erratic each time, until she passed the forties. Then Mr. Homfray hobbled out to a chair on the edge of the lawn, and she had to play twice more in order to pleasure him. (41 and 43.)

Cross and fatigued with all the bending she wandered to another part of the garden, and found Mrs. Homfray, wearing an irregular hat and thick leather gloves, snipping off dead roses with a large pair of gardening scissors.

"You see," said Mrs. Homfray, "we are not entertaining you. But it's an excellent thing to be rather bored sometimes."

"Can I help you?"

"Certainly not. You'd never forgive me if I allowed you to."

Miss Clame did not press the point.

"We were to have had a little tennis party this afternoon," Mrs. Homfray went on. "Lady Cecilia Remington was bringing her daughters over, and I asked Lady Browne too. But the Remingtons can't come and I've heard nothing from Lady Browne, so I fear nobody's coming at all. We're very haphazard over our invitations. Unfortunately there aren't any young men in the neighbourhood. Geoffrey Remington's the only one, and he's in Switzerland, I believe."

"Oh, please don't trouble about me," said Miss Clame. "I love to vegetate." And she withdrew to the kitchen-garden in order to be alone with her thoughts and the cabbage-whites that flopped about like soap-suds.

"Shall I take up butterfly-collecting?" Miss Clame thought. "Would it be a relief to me? I seem to need something to take me out of myself. All this waiting, this living from day to day, is very trying. I wonder if by collecting things one unfits oneself for society? It would be marvellous if one could put one's higher faculties away, like money into war-savings certificates, and bring them out when required, with interest—one's higher and also some of one's lower faculties. It's such a pity that one can't do anything with them when there's no scope for them. I believe I had this thought last time I was here. This place must be very sterile. Such a pity, because it is a charming spot. I could spend a delightful honeymoon here. We would be in and out of the water all day long, basking on the bank and dressing one anothers' limbs in chains of daisies and poppies and roses. How should I look, I wonder? I must try some-time—perhaps to-night, if I feel very romantic, when they've all gone to bed. Miss Dorlip, if she saw me, would have a seizure. My trouble is, I'm too correct. I blame Aunt Dawes for much. I suffer from Chinese feet in the soul—strapped too tightly in infancy, it hurts me to let myself go. That's why Jenny Sale thinks me a prude. (Fool! I could shock her with my little finger.) And people like the Homfrays think me eccentric. I have a way of doing what I want to do so unnaturally. It must be some guilt-complex. If only I could cease to appear a naughty child. There must be some way of overcoming the trait. Shall I ask Miss Dorlip how to become genuinely abandoned?"

In the distance a bell tinkled for lunch. Miss Clame turned towards the house. Decidedly the fresh air made one numb. She had not even a good appetite. She must be a little below par to be so affected by the change of air. She de-cided to take more exercise after lunch. She would feel all the better for it in London. It might even give her a really beautiful com-plexion.

After lunch, Mr. Homfray went to his study for a nap, and Mrs. Homfray, who had caught a touch of the sun while busied with the roses, lay down in her room, and asked Miss Clame if she would mind having a solitary tea. Apparently Mr. Homfray's naps lasted not infrequently till dinner. Miss Clame went upstairs herself, unmindful of her resolve. For twenty minutes she read, and then played patience, but she was restless and the garden tempted her out again. She next played four rounds of croquet, but her scores were so bad (41, 39, 44, 45) that she felt quite alarmed. Perhaps she was smoking too many cigarettes? At all events, she could not concentrate. That was her trouble, lack of concentration. She was too much absorbed in herself. She was an *introvert*. That was the word. Henceforward she would correct that quality by paying a more continuous attention to externals. That very minute she would begin. She would walk down one of the paths and notice minutely and accurately everything that met her eye.

" Grass of several different kinds. The lawn is chiefly composed of moss and clover and plantains. In the border on my left a shrub, species unknown to me. Another shrub (the flowering currant, perhaps, though not in flower). Another shrub—the kind that you see in pots outside inferior boarding-houses by the sea, with untidy children playing round them and upsetting pails of sandy sea-water, while their shrimping-nets are left hanging on the iron railings—Sh ! "

She paused, horrified to find how quickly she had strayed from fact to fancy. Why was it that what was before her eyes was so much duller than what was absent ? Had she been at the sea-side, it would have been delightful to picture the garden at Elfindale. She continued :

" A pine tree. A laurel ; another laurel with a differently shaped leaf. Two peacock butter-flies at their dalliance. (Cut out the words ' at their dalliance.') A pine tree, a chestnut tree, a cluster of orange rambler roses trailing from a post. A big tree—is it a mountain-ash ?—covered with red berries. A silver birch. Some untidy marguerites and stunted antirrhinums. Another mountain-ash, with yellower berries than those on the first one. A flowering currant. Will the path never end ? "

She paused in her cataloguing and wondered if tea was nearly ready. Her watch had stopped. That was a bad sign. If she could count twenty rose trees between where she was and the privet-hedge, everything would be all right. One, two, three. At the edge of the lawn was a circular bed containing about thirty-one China roses. It was too easy a " test " to be conclusive.

She fetched her Saint-Simon from the house,

and took it to a seat in the sunken garden—a soothing place with a fountain in the centre and stone-paving walks threading through beds of choice roses. She read for some time, imagining herself to be in one of those old deserted parks which she had never really seen, though they had long been one of her symbols of paradise. Then she looked up and saw a long and highly coloured snake sunning itself a few feet from where she was.

Much as she loved all insects (even ants and beetles), she had a horror of snakes, and she left the sunken garden on tip-toe with suppressed screams, vowing that she would never go there again.

After tea, the maid brought word that Mrs. Homfray was feeling worse rather than better, and begged to be excused from dinner. Mr. Homfray had gone in the motor to Maidenhead to see his doctor and one or two friends, and had arranged to dine there at the club. Meanwhile Miss Dorlip had telephoned that she was staying for a bean-feast of some kind at St. Gradimir's, and would not be back till nearly midnight.

" Fate seems to insist on my being left alone," thought Miss Clame. " I must commit no indiscretion." She went and sat on the lawn which the attentions of Winckworths had made so tropical earlier in the year. All the palm trees had been replaced by roses. Apparently the Homfrays had lost their interest in the exotic ; indeed, their garden could hardly have been more commonplace, except for the part tenanted by the snake.

Finally, deciding that nothing could possibly be more boring and depressing than the country, she went to her bedroom, lay down on the bed and fell asleep.

XVIII

SHE was awakened by a little gong beaten dis-
creetly outside her door. Disturbed in a delightful dream, she was peevish. She had not
even time to change her dress. But why change ?
Only the doddering Mr. Homfray might see her,
and she did not wish to inflame him. After a
rapid wash, she went down and ate a solitary
meal. By the time she had finished, the sun was
setting and the tall evergreens stood out against
a lurid sky with a majesty which they altogether
lacked by day. A hot scent drifted in through
the window. The healthy and irritating breeze
which had been blowing in the morning had died
down, and the air was heavy and thick. It was
a real summer evening.

Miss Clame went out into the garden, and the
bats flew in circles round her. In the cedar tree
an owl was sitting. (An owl, says Josephus,
appeared before Herod Agrippa when he was
eaten of worms.) A moth struck her in the face.
" It is enchanting," she thought, and remembered
how Ippolita in D'Annunzio's *Il Trionfo della*

Morte, had pinned a living moth in her hair. " I feel at one with the shadows," she continued. " O roses, O syringa ! " The perfume overcame her. " I must make the most of this night," she said to herself. " It's impressions are very splendid ! " Then she reached the river, which lapped gently and perpetually against the stone bank. " O river," she apostrophised it, not having read Paul Valéry for nothing. " What a place for a *liebestod* ! "

In the gloom a black and white figure approached her. It was the maid, carrying a white piece of paper.

" If you please, Miss, would you kindly read this message ? It's come by telephone from Moulton Bassett, and I don't know, I'm sure, whether to tell the mistress or not."

The maid was much agitated, and the words " Moulton Bassett " had kindled Miss Clame's curiosity.

" Why, what does it say ? " she asked.

" I'd rather you read it, if you please, Miss," said the maid with a sob.

" Is it bad news ? Is Lady Cecilia ill ? "

But the maid said nothing and walked back into the house. Miss Clame followed her. It was too dark to read outside.

" Telegram has arrived this morning saying

146

Mr. Geoffrey and Miss Betty Green-Travers killed in motor accident at Cauax yesterday evening."

The words were evidently written by the servant who took down the message. The paper was a sheet torn from the " telephone block " in the hall. Miss Clame looked at it for a long time. Then she said, " Are you sure it was Cauax ? C-a-u-a-x ? "

" I don't know, Miss, I don't know," and the maid burst into a harangue mingled with tears. She had been in service once with Lady Cecilia. Miss Clame heard nothing except her own voice saying mechanically, " Tell Mr. Homfray when he comes in. Don't tell Mrs. Homfray. Tell Mr. Homfray when he comes in . . ."

Still repeating the sentence she walked away, and went methodically to the place on the river bank at which she had received the message. The water lapped soothingly at the mossy stones and fascinated her as if her will-power were oozing into the stream and she could watch it borne eastward to the sea by the current.

Then she turned suddenly, and, like a top lashed into a bizarre vitality, darted round the rose-bushes, round the trees, over the flower-beds, leapt on to a little stone wall, ran along it with unhesitating steps, passed, a pale lightning flash, through the sunken garden at the end of it, over more flower-beds, round the cedar tree, on to the verandah, into the hall, upstairs into her bedroom, where she tore off her clothes and put on a shabby blue bathing-dress. Then she raced out of the house again, straight to the river and plunged in.

For a while she swam down-stream with big mechanical strokes. Then, as the gracious coldness of the water penetrated all the surface of her body, she became filled with an ecstasy, and swam on faster and faster as if to reach a gigantic water-fall which would fling her straight to another world. Onward she swept beneath overhanging branches, past meadows, cottages, hedges, every minute more at one with the stream. It seemed to her as if the mouth of the river would come all too soon. " In a short while," she thought, " I shall reach the outer factories. As I raise my head I shall see the lights of London rising in a huge column (the epitome of all its busy follies) in front of me. Gradually the stream will widen and I shall be carried under the great bridges, Hammersmith Bridge, Putney Bridge, Westminster Bridge, London Bridge, the Tower Bridge (whose arms will rise in a salute as I approach), into the immense docks, a dolphin playing round monstrous keels. Down the estuary I shall go, past the landing-stage at Tilbury and a last wave of human hands, past the light-ships beckoning me with twinkling green, Nore, Mouse, Girdler, Tongue, East Goodwin, Sandettié, Ruytingen, West Hinder, Wandelaar (from which, glancing to the right, I shall see the Casino at Ostend glittering in its midnight splendour). Or it may be that I shall be carried northward past the Sunk light-ship and the Outer Gabbard along the coast of Norway towards the Pole, till at length I shall feel the frozen sea closing over me in a solid arch of green, and I myself shall be embalmed for ever in a coffin of green crystal, while overhead the snow will patter down, building me a white canopy mountains high. . . ."

At this point she ceased to think at all, and was recalled to her senses by water in the mouth and nose. She was too tired to swim further, and climbed out of the river on to a soft grass bank. A big beery man with his shirt-sleeves rolled up (publican, coachman, blacksmith ?) stood watching her, and, when she rose, seized her, dripping as she was, in his arms.

" Let me go," she said dreamily. " Let me dry myself."

" I'll dry yer," he said, and began to do so with his big hands.

Then she screamed, hit his nose with her elbow, and scampered along the bank towards Elfindale. The man followed her for a few steps, then slipped and fell sprawling on the ground, where he remained laughing with loud unconcern. Miss Clame glanced backwards, as if half minded to help him to his feet, thought better of it, and hurried homewards along the edge of the river. She had to clamber through hedges and over railings, and once a couple in a boat looked at her with surprise. But it was not really so far to Elfindale, and she soon reached a spot on the bank opposite that from which she had taken her plunge. She swam across to the garden, and crept into the house up to her room, praying that she would not meet a maid. Then she dried herself quickly, dressed, and crept downstairs again.

By the telephone in the hall she saw the message from Moulton Bassett, but hurried past it as though it were an irritating trifle of which she did not wish to be reminded. She was a little noisy opening the front door, but escaped from the house and garden without being seen. Then she walked for about an hour and a half and reached Maidenhead, where she found a taxi, and told the man to drive her to 52 Beam Square, London (east of Tottenham Court Road).

The moment the car started, she felt so cold and tired that she fell into a stupor, and never noticed the bonfires of the slaughtered cattle in the fields which bordered the road.

At length, after many an intermittent doze, she realised that they had reached Hyde Park Corner.   Looking out of the right-hand window she saw a taxi coming from the direction of Victoria Station.   Inside it was the ghost of Geoffrey Remington, holding a tennis-racket. He looked through her rather than at her.   Then they passed.

At Beam Square she paid the driver, fumbling with numb fingers in her bag for the last six-pence—so near was she to not having enough—unlocked the front door and went upstairs to bed. Cold as she was, she had no energy to light the geyser and fill herself a hot-water bottle.

XIX

Miss Clame stretched out her hand for her watch, and found that it was half-past ten. Something was very wrong, but she could not quite decide what it was. She ached all over, and when she raised her head, felt dizzy. She longed for some tea, but unless she made it herself, there was no one to get it for her ; for Anna had been given a holiday, as it was expected that no one would be in residence.

A quarter of an hour passed, and as her consciousness increased, she felt more unwell each moment. She dared not take her temperature, so hot was she, and at the same time so cold. But an effort must be made to get some tea. She got out of bed and tottered in an old but thick dressing-gown and down-at-heel bedroom slippers to the gas ring. There was no bread in the flat, though there should be a tin of biscuits in the dining-room — and some chocolates. At the thought of them she was seized with nausea and symptoms of collapse, and before the water boiled, turned off the gas and stumbled back to bed.

" What have I done ? " she moaned. " What is the matter with me ? " It was terrible to be so lonely, to have nobody within miles (anywhere, perhaps) who cared for her at all. (Surely in an hour's time she would feel better.) It must be a bad chill. Very few people really cared for her. Mavina probably had some affection. Somehow she had not troubled about real friends. She had gone in for hard metallic people. When one is ill, it is the homely people who count. (How terrible to be reduced to homely people ! How degrading illness was !) Absolute isolation ; not even a charwoman about to give her some tea in a chipped enamel mug. Something must be done. . . .

She lay quietly on her back, looking at a swarm of little flies moving round the electric-light pendant. That was better. Imagine the ceiling a map—those cracks railway lines, the brown mark a range of hills. Starting at the west end, one would go eastward, northward, northward . . .

A heavy van rumbled through the square, and all was peaceful again. " I can't stay here like this till night," she thought with sudden terror. " I can't spend a night alone." What was to be done ? She could telephone to a registry office for a help, a charwoman, even a companion.

None of them would know what to do. They could only ask to whom they should telegraph—Mavina, Deevie. The pains in her chest, back, and head became so violent that she could not think at all.

She awoke as a clock was striking twelve. For the moment, she was less overcome. While she had strength, she thought, she must do something. She put on the dressing-gown again, and wrapped herself in the eiderdown, and went out to the telephone in the hall, rang up a doctor whom she had not consulted for two years, asked him to come round at once, struggled to the flat-door, which she unlocked, and back to bed.

He would, of course, send for a trained nurse. She was ill, and might as well be comfortable. It would be something to be petted, have the pillows straightened, one's hair brushed, face washed, to have no responsibility about oneself.

As she fell asleep again she developed a great internal garrulity. " I don't know what it is," she said to herself. " I see no reason why I shouldn't make a success of things. But I always seem to have more to contend with than any one else—or else other people take things more lightly. I am really too serious. That's why I appear to be so flippant—why different people think such different things about me.

154

I'm not really one of the flippant type. Perhaps
I have tried to fit myself into a wrong groove.
I've been bothered all the time by my ideals, my
spiritual outlook. That's what it is. Earnest
women like Miss Dorlip, religious people, clergy-
men, have nothing like my long vision. If only
I could express myself so that people should all
see it. I've tried, I suppose, in my life, and
people see it as a lot of little bubbles of excitement, bursting every minute into nothing. It's
the feeling of getting away that I wanted to
bring out — not destroying, but being free.
There was that time—(if only I could have
analysed it so as to have it ready to explain to
people)—when I felt that what I wanted was very
near—on a railway journey, when the window
passed some hills with rich trees growing luxuri-
antly up the slopes, with a break in the centre and
the sky looking like an immense lake stretching
out to the horizon. Moving, not standing still,
made it so good. It's like the effect of mixture
that Proust says he found in Elstir's pictures—
the sea more like land than the land, which re-
sembled the sky. It's being hemmed in by
nothing, that I'm after—not being bothered by
weak sympathies or blustering opaque enthu-
siasms. I always have loved to be free—not
desolate or lonely—(the middle of a large plain

would be as bad as a dungeon)—but having no roots, not being tied down to anything. I have loved dissociating myself from things, severing connections, doing things for the last time—(not ceasing to do things altogether). It may, of course, be the fear of the gloomy little ending to most lives, the dark room, the smell of antiseptic, the dim voices, the clergyman and an undignified repentance, the coffin waiting in the passage. . . .

" I love to move from thing to thing, to have changes, to be bigger than my surroundings, to break away from them. Passionless is the wrong word. Careless is better—not to be interfered with by pain or suffering or unkindness or any kind of convention. Something very beautiful, serene, limitless but varied, like the background to ' La Gioconda '—(that gives me the feeling)— like the second act of Strauss's *Ariadne*, exquisitely and remotely beautiful, not primitive or elemental, but calm, classical (yet freer than a classic), passionless. No, passionless is the wrong word.

" If one could cease to be bothered with society and the way it is outraged, opinions of any sort, laws of nature, any kind of laws ! If life could be like a dream, and one could fall out of the window like Jezebel but without being damaged, climb the church steeple without effort, reach

Buenos Aires by walking across the Park, drive
a submarine through the underground and emerge
amongst the flying gold-fish of the Crystal Palace,
while a little engine made of string pulled the
Kremlin (like a loose tooth attached to a door-
handle by a piece of cotton) out of Moscow. . . .
Non-existence is an awful thought. It is not
that. I want to live and appreciate everything
without being tied down to anything. I want
to live and even to hurt myself without being
distressed at it. As it is, we can only enjoy half
the possible sensations. (At all events I have
had my heart cut out, painted gold, and replaced
without an anaesthetic by a cricket eleven dressed
in bathing costumes.) That is why my friends
tend to dislike me when they know me well. In
my universe there is no room for two. Yet the
universe is badly made. Have I made it?

" You remember, Geoffrey, how during that
voyage to India of ours we used to stand after tea
on deck out of the way of the smoke, and watch
the foam we churned up stretching like a railway
line behind us among those green islands, winding
in and out, until after twenty-four hours the whole
sea had gone round the earth, and we were where
we had started (but a day younger), and I said,
laughing, ' As I'm the elder, Geoffrey, I shall soon

see the time when you were not yet born ! ' And you said, ' Yes. The sun which seems to be red to you is golden to me. Twelve hours of the twenty-four have gone already. Though we face the same direction, we are looking different ways. I can see no islands.' And I said, ' But we are still passing them. We have been threading our way through them for the last month.' ' No,' you said, ' there are no islands there for me. I only see immense clouds and a long stretch of pale sea flowing away from us.' And I was terrified, and pulled you by the shoulder and the ears and told you to come away from the deck which was so dangerous for you, down to our cabin. But you stood so still and looked so hard at the pale water that you might have been seeing nothing at all. . . ."

XX

THE hot sun enlarged the blisters on the dark green painted railings of " Zamborina " (Ladbroke Grove) and even created new ones. Miss Gweller, casting critical glances about her, ascended the steep flight of steps and pressed a small bell labelled " Inquiries " (black letters on a white enamel ground). After a long delay, the door was opened by Sister Kezia Schultze, who rubbed her hands with a piece of rag.

" I wish," said Miss Gweller, " to see Miss Clame."

" That is impossible," said Sister Kezia.

" And why ? " asked Miss Gweller. " I thought the excellent habit of early rising had its stronghold in medical circles. Do you mean to tell me, nurse, that the patient's room is not yet done ? "

" In any event," said Sister Kezia, " we never permit visitors to see patients before two o'clock in the afternoon, unless there is great urgency, the doctor consents, and the visitor is a near relative. But as regards Miss Clame, I fear that she is far too ill to receive anybody. The fever shows no signs of abating. She is delirious. Are you a relative?"

"Miss Clame," said Miss Gweller, "is an intimate friend of mine. Here is my card. I trust that the patient is receiving every attention, that her room has a cheerful aspect, that the food here is good—above the average standard of nursing homes."

"I repeat, madam," said Sister Kezia, with more of a foreign accent than before, "that Miss Clame is gravely ill. Eating is for her beyond all question. I will place your name upon the list of inquirers, up to now a small one. More I cannot do."

"Remember," said Miss Gweller as if in warning, "I shall call again soon. By the way, should Lord Underbody's car call for me here, will you tell the chauffeur that as I was unable to see the patient, I did not wait for the car but went straight on."

"Went where?" asked Sister Kezia.

"Straight on," said Miss Gweller with a jerk of the left shoulder as she turned to descend the steps, "straight on. Straight on . . ."

Sister Kezia hummed the air "Land of Hope and Glory," and closed the door.

Mrs. Homfray, having rung the bell labelled " Service," was received by Jane.

" I have come to inquire about—to see, if possible—a Miss Clame . . ."

" Kindly step into the waiting-room, please'm, and I'll call nurse."

The waiting-room was so narrow that one could barely sit at the table. But there was nothing on the table except a tattered copy of *Pearson's Magazine*, April 1922, and a pocket medical encyclopaedia. Mrs. Homfray opened the latter at " Yellow Fever," and read the words : " Then the terrible black vomit sets in." She closed the book hurriedly, and unwrapped a crystal globe which she had brought with her covered in several layers of tissue paper. Then she waited for twenty-five minutes, till Nurse Jackson (Norah) came in.

" So sorry to keep you waiting all this time," she said, putting a gushing emphasis on all the unimportant words, " but you haven't an idea how rushed we are. Lem'me see. Miss Clame, wasn't it ? I'm afraid she's very poorly, very poorly indeed. Delirious. Being given oxygen. No one except a relative can be admitted. But no doubt you'd like to leave a card ? "

" My name is Mrs. Homfray. I fear I have

forgotten my card-case. I will telephone again
this afternoon. Had I known how serious it
was, I should of course have come up from the
country before. I feel almost responsible. You
see—it was while staying with us that she com-
mitted the imprudence. . . . Her costume was
found wringing wet. . . . But, nurse, I ask you
to promise me this. The moment your patient
regains consciousness, take this globe to her and
tell her to look at it fixedly first with the right eye
and then with the left eye and to say " All goes
well" about a dozen times. The result, I can
assure you, is marvellous. Everything rests with
her own will. We can but hope. May I rely
upon you for this ? "

" Yes, that will be *quite* all right." (It was the
tone in which they tell you that your ticket is
available for three intermediate stations excluding
Little Bumpton and Amiens, while its validity
is extendable from forty-five to fifty-eight days
on payment of one and three-quarter per cent of
the original price.)

" I'm greatly obliged to you," said Mrs.
Homfray.

" And you'll ring us up this afternoon ? "

" Yes, indeed. And of course, if there's anything I can do . . ."

" Quite so, we'll let you know."

" And you won't forget? I'm sure you won't. Good morning."

" *Good* day."

General Osgood had already telephoned twice. When he had climbed the steps and had begun to wonder about the bells, Jane opened the front door. He handed her a large bouquet of flowers. " They're labelled," he said huskily and walked away.

Nurse Jackson had from a window seen his fine figure disappearing, and hurried downstairs.

" What's the good of you," she said witheringly, " trying to give news of the patients? Show the visitors into the waiting-room, as I've told you before."

" Please, nurse," said Jane, " he didn't ask me." But Nurse Jackson, like jesting Pilate, set no store by answers.

Sir William Rampie was far the smartest doctor who sent patients to " Zamborina," and Mrs. Burrington expressed her obligation to him by seeing him off herself when he had done his rounds. With a little wave he got into his Napier and drove away. Mrs. Burrington stood framed in the doorway enjoying the sunshine, and flushed with faint success. (It seemed likely that Lady Smerder would make a long stay.)

Then she saw four young people walking rather vulgarly up the road. She disapproved of them instantly, and when she realised that they were pausing at " Zamborina," was about to close the door. But she was too late.

" Half a mo'," shouted Stanley Dalrymple, beckoning her to wait.

And he was joined by Jenny Sale, Deevie, and Hilton Grownlow.

" Of all the gloomy places," said Jenny with feeling.

" Could we see the person in charge here ? " asked Deevie.

" Have you an Inquiry Department ? " said Grownlow.

" I shall be obliged," said Mrs. Burrington acidly, " if you will speak in lower tones. This is a private nursing home. I am the Matron. What can I do for you ? "

Jenny Sale was a perfect lady. " We wish," she said in her special voice, " to see Miss Clame."

" You mean, you have come to inquire about Miss Clame. Perhaps you will kindly step into the waiting-room. I must ask the other lady and the two gentlemen to take a stroll up the road. Our accommodation is not sufficient for them."

" But we are all friends of Miss Clame's," said Deevie.

" This gentleman here," said Jenny, pointing to Grownlow, " is connected with the medical profession. He may wish to ask you some questions."

" If he does," Mrs. Burrington replied, " I shall certainly not answer them. I cannot believe his connection with the medical profession is very big, or he would have more notion of medical etiquette."

She smacked her lips. Grownlow reddened sheepishly. Then Dalrymple like an invader mounted the steps, planted himself in front of the matron, and said very loudly, " Look here, we all want to see Miss Clame. Please don't let's have any more humbug. Can we see her or not, and if not, why not ? "

Mrs. Burrington lost her temper.

" For the Lord's sake," she said, " don't shout like that. You can't see Miss Clame, any of you. She's very seriously ill indeed. She's not expected to recover."

There was a silence, and Deevie, who was standing behind Dalrymple, nestled up to him, took his hand and whimpered.

" Oh, Stan," she said, " think of poor little Lydd. It's awful."

He squeezed her arm, and whispered, " There, there. Don't cry—poppet ! " It was an erotic joke between them, and Deevie began to giggle through her sobs.

" It can't be true," said Jenny. " In pneumonia the crisis doesn't—when does the crisis come, Hil ? "

" I have given you all the information in my power," said Mrs. Burrington. " I shall be obliged if you will leave this place in an orderly fashion. Good day."

She closed the door firmly and strutted upstairs, a little surprised that so lady-like a patient as Miss Clame should have friends who drank.

It was about six o'clock when Reggie Muswell arrived, carrying a few very good roses—cheaper and more delicate than several very bad ones. He had learnt his little speech of inquiry by heart and hoped to escape as soon as he had delivered it. The last thing he wished was to be allowed an interview ; indeed, the sight of an invalid always made him feel faint.

He was greeted by Nurse Jackson, who had several smiles for him. But he looked at the ground instead of at her, and said, " I have brought these flowers for Miss Clame. (My card is attached to them.) Can you tell me how she is ? I suppose it is rather late for me to ask to see her ? ''

" I'm awfully sorry," she said, " but you can't see her. It is too late—besides, she's really too ill to see any one. We've had to turn away quite a number to-day. But I'll put your flowers with the others, and keep your card—so that'll be quite all right." (Again the railway ticket voice.)

" Oh, thank you so much," said Reggie. " I'm dreadfully sorry you haven't good news. But one can't hope to get well in a day, can one ? And I'm sure you're all doing everything for her that can be done. Good-bye. Thank you so much."

He hurried away, and Nurse Jackson, a little grieved that he had closed the conversation so abruptly, went to the nurses' room and put the flowers in a vase.

" What name, 'm, please ? " asked Jane.
" Mrs. Dawes. I have called to inquire about my niece, who, I understand, is an inmate here. Her name is Miss Clame. At least it was when I last heard of her. She may have changed it now, for all I know."

" Will you kindly step into the waiting-room, please'm ? "

" I will, but I trust I shall not be forced to wait long."

After a few minutes Sister Kezia (disturbed while having her supper) appeared before the visitor.

" I am," said Mrs. Dawes, " the aunt of your patient, Miss Clame. I came as soon as I heard of her trouble, though her conduct to me has been far from endearing. I suppose it is safely over ? "

" It ? "

" I mean, of course, is it a boy or a girl ? Or perhaps it is still-born ? That would indeed be a mercy."

" I fear we are at cross-purposes, Mrs. Dawes. If you are speaking of Miss Clame, I do not understand your questions."

" Sur-'y they are plain enough. I understand that my niece came here some days ago for an urgent and delicate reason. If she has married the man, of course, it is all to the good, though a marriage of this sort could hardly be described as made in Heaven. You have a Miss Clame here ? "

" Yes. A Miss Lydia Clame."

" Quite so. Is the case under your own observation ? "

" All our cases come under my observation, madam."

" Well, then, you should know if it's over or not. I hope the ordeal was not, or is not being painful."

" Miss Clame, I regret to say, has suffered great pain, but now——"

" You do not, I trust, on any account use ' Twilight Sleep '—a dangerous proceeding of which I disapprove on many grounds."

" Surely, madam, you labour under a singular misapprehension. Twilight sleep has reference only to maternity cases."

" Do you mean to say that my niece is not a maternity case ? "

" Far from it, madam. She has never— pardon—she is a—a spinster in every sense of that word."

" I can hardly believe my ears."

" Really, madam, there is nothing very strange in what I say."

" After her loose life . . . in the midst of her temptations . . . I am amazed. You must ex- cuse me. My information has misled me. What, then, is her trouble ? "

" She is suffering from double pneumonia and other complications resulting from a severe and neglected chill, contracted, we are told, while bathing. Her plight is most grave. She is at present unconscious, and we fear that little can be done for her. You will no doubt wish to see her."

"Indeed, I do not. If she is unconscious, the sight of her would be painful to me and useless to her. I trust that your pessimism is unfounded, nurse. Here is my card. I am staying at Wesley's Hotel, De Vere Gardens. I have written my telephone number in the corner. If my niece asks for me—or you have bad news—perhaps you will communicate with me. I shall be there all this evening. Indeed, I must go now, or I shall be late for dinner."

And she, too, went away.

At a quarter to nine it was growing quite dark. (The nights at the end of July are longer than in June.) Geoffrey Remington, dressed in his light snuff suit and swinging a malacca cane, walked up the deserted road to "Zamborina." Little birds had been whispering, and though (like Siegfried ˉbefore he tasted the dragon's blood) he was not very clever at interpreting their meaning, he had gathered enough to feel that there was a difficulty somewhere. Again he went over the confused story that had made him so ridiculous, the stock phrases of it coming disconnectedly into his mind. . . . " The wretched car did turn a somersault, you know. . . . Our last evening. . . . Luckily Betty and I were only shaken. . . . Thought it would be such a lark to arrive at the hotel and find them all looking as blue as thrushes' eggs. . . . Should have got back in ten minutes after we'd sent the message if the tin-pot funicular hadn't jammed. . . . Telephone place closed down. . . . There we were, stuck for two solid hours. . . . Got back and the damage was done. . . . Millions of telegrams sent off everywhere, most of them held up for forty-eight hours. . . . Pretty poor joke it turned out. . . ." Well, there was no need to tell the whole tale again. It would do if he said they weren't killed or anything—and of course inquired . . .

Arriving at " Zamborina " he lit his pipe, went up the steps and rang the " Inquiries " bell. Sister Kezia was in the passage, about to go out, and opened the door. Her mood was less professional than usual. When Geoffrey saw her, he took off his hat, holding it with his stick in his right hand. With his left hand he held his pipe.

" Er—" he said, " is Miss Clame staying here ? "

Sister Kezia said nothing, but peered with her large moon of a face (a moon seen on a foggy winter's night in London by a tired traveller coming out of the last tube) at Geoffrey, while her eyes, absorbing his fair hair, tanned complexion and blue eyes, clouded. Then, as he was about to repeat his question or ask another, she laid a finger on her lips.

For three minutes they looked at one another as if each of them were hypnotised by the other. Then at last Geoffrey understood, bowed his head in acquiescence, and walked out into the road. When he had passed the house, he put the pipe back in his mouth. As for his hat, he carried it absent-mindedly in his hand till he reached home.

THE END